14: LEAH'S NIGHTMARE

When I woke up I was sweating. I sat bolt upright in bed and waited for the horrible banal little nursery tune that was penetrating my skull to go away. Staring into the darkness I could still see Anna Slater playing her violin and my own eyes staring out of an ashen face. I snapped the bedside light on and took deep breaths. I'd had that awful nightmare again…

Also in the Café Club series by Ann Bryant

Have you read?
Go For It, Fen!
Leah Discovers Boys
Luce and the Weird Kid
Jaimini and the Web of Lies
Andy the Prisoner
Tash's Secrets
Fen's Revenge
Leah in Trouble
Luce's Big Mistake
Jaimini and the Mystery of Evi Bligh
Andy in the Dark
Tash and the Fortune-Teller
Fen Gets Jealous

Look out for:
Luce Finds Her Hero

14: LEAH'S NIGHTMARE

Ann Bryant

For my great friend, Sue Mahon,
and Paddy, Patrick, Abi and Hannah

Scholastic Children's Books,
Commonwealth House, 1–19 New Oxford Street,
London WC1A 1NU, UK
a division of Scholastic Ltd
London ~ New York ~ Toronto ~ Sydney ~ Auckland

First published by Scholastic Ltd, 1998

ISBN 0 590 19748 7

Typeset by TW Typesetting, Midsomer Norton, Somerset

Printed by Cox & Wyman Ltd, Reading, Berks.

10 9 8 7 6 5 4 3 2 1

Chapter 1

Hi, I'm Leah. My friends call me "the musician". I generally call myself "the worrier", but right now I'd say I'm "the dream freak"!

I've just had *the* dream again, only this time it seemed more real than ever. I dreamt that Anna Slater, the famous violinist, turned up at the café and seemed to know me. I suppose she's about forty-something really, but in my dream she's more like thirty and very beautiful. She's got long, long fingers, lovely slim, floaty arms and she dresses in floaty clothes, too. In the dream she wants me to accompany her on the piano and she gives me the music and although the music looks really difficult I know I'll be able to play it, and I'm really proud and excited that I've been given the honour of accompanying the great Anna Slater.

Then we start playing in front of this vast

audience, and Anna Slater is naturally playing her violin part really brilliantly, but my fingers won't work properly and my part is coming out all wrong. In fact, it's so bad that the audience are squirming in their seats. Then the worst bit of the dream starts. You see, what nobody realizes is that I'm wearing an earpiece, and someone is whispering into it. A male voice is counting down slowly, and he's told me that this is the count-down to a bomb going off in my piano! And I know I've got to escape but I daren't run away, because the concert is too big and important and I can't let Anna Slater down. I can feel the blood draining from my face until my face doesn't feel human at all.

The voice in my earpiece starts singing this simple little tune and my fingers just can't help playing it, so while Anna Slater is playing her fantastically complicated and wonderful violin part, my fingers are helplessly drumming out this hateful little tune. And the voice in my earpiece gets down to ten and I *know* I've got to escape, and I'm trying to run away, but my legs won't move. They're like lead, and however much I struggle I can't get away. But it's not the bomb I'm trying to get away from. It's the hateful, stupid little tune. By this time I'm panicking, and I'm desperate and crying and I use every fibre in my body to force myself to move, and the voice says "three ... two ... one ..." and the bomb goes off! The explosion smashes through the silly little tune...

And I wake up.

I'm lying here right now, heart still beating loudly and my whole body exhausted, but I daren't go back to sleep in case the nightmare begins again, so I'm trying to fill my mind with nice, normal thoughts. I'm going through all my friends and picturing them sitting at the café where we all work in Cableden. This café is run by the aunt of one of my friends. Because we're all only thirteen our parents don't approve of us working more than once a week, so we all take turns. There are six of us, and we work Monday to Friday for a couple of hours each day after school, then Saturday all afternoon. We have this rota so that we can work different days. That way we all get a chance to do Saturday when the hours are longer and you make more money.

It's great working at the café. You feel really grown up, and you get to meet all sorts of people. Unfortunately not everyone who comes into the café is nice... Oh, no! I've let that woman, Anna Slater, from my dream, come back into my head. Quick, Leah! Think of something else. Andy. Think of Andy. Right.

Andy Sorrell is my best friend. She's very small and slim with extremely short dark hair and big brown eyes. Her real name is Agnès which you pronounce *Ann-yes* because she's half French. Her mum is French. Her dad's English, but works in France. Andy is the daring one of us. There's nothing that she wouldn't dare to do. If she's scared of anything it's her dad, because he's quite a hard sort of man. He terrifies me, but I suppose I get scared and worried more easily than anyone else in my group of friends. So, you see, Andy and I are completely different from each other, and not just in character. I've got long, blonde hair down to my waist and bluey-grey eyes.

Fen, short for Fenella Brooks, is the one who started our whole Café Club going in the first place. It's her aunt Jan who manages the café. Fen is the ambitious one. She always seems to be searching for something, and she usually gets what she wants. She's quite tall and thin with shoulder-length, light brown hair and freckles. She wears jeans nearly all the time and is very fit and sporty.

Tash, short for Natasha Johnston, is Fen's best friend. Tash is the peacemaker. If I'm the worst worrier in the group, Tash is the second worst, and she and I often find ourselves hanging back while our best friends go hurtling forwards. Tash has got fairly short, dark hair and very dark twinkling eyes. She's the kindest person I know and always thinks about others before herself.

She hates it when anyone isn't friends with anyone else, and is often the person who quietly sorts out arguments and things.

Jaimini Riva, which you pronounce *Jay-m-nee Reever*, is the brainy one. I think she's the beautiful one, as well. Because her father is black and her mother white, Jaimini has got the most lovely coffee-coloured skin and deep black eyes. Her hair is black too, and long, like mine.

Luce, short for Lucy Edmunson, is Jaimini's best friend. She's also the crazy one. I often wish I could be like Luce, and crash happily through life having a great time. I once told Jaimini that, and she said, "Thank goodness you're not, Leah. Two of you would be too much to bear!" Poor Jaimini is always having to keep an eye on Luce to make sure she's not acting too outrageously.

Actually, acting is something at which Luce is fantastic. She can become a different character in seconds. She has a terrific talent. Luce has got wild, strawberry-blonde curls and a big smile. She often wears make-up and flashy earrings, and the latest thing is a different coloured nail varnish for every nail. We're not allowed to wear nail varnish at school, so Luce spends most of the day trying to keep her hands out of sight, which can't be easy when she's writing things down. I never wear nail varnish because of playing the piano and the violin. Nail varnish and practising don't mix!

* * *

"I had that nightmare again last night."

"Oh, Leah, you didn't, did you?"

That was Tash, who looked so sorry for me. Looking round at the others, I saw they all wore the same sympathetic expression. We were sitting on the grass by the netball courts, as far away on the school premises that anyone is allowed to venture. We're overlooked by the staffroom window, but we don't mind because it's a long way off, and the teachers are more interested in drinking coffee than looking out at us. That's why we often come down here at break-times. No one ever disturbs us. All the same, I keep my eye on the staffroom window because I hate getting told off, so if I catch sight of one of the teachers looking even remotely disapprovingly through the window at us, I quickly tell the others, and we sit up straight like the best behaved girls in the school. Our school is called Cableden Comprehensive. It's a big school, but on the whole a friendly one. I'm quite happy here.

"How many times have you had that dream?" Tash was asking me.

"I don't know. About five."

"And can't you think of any reason why you had it in the first place? Did you see Anna Slater on television or something?"

I shook my head and tried for the hundredth

time to think of why it could be that I kept having the same dream.

"You've got a poster of Anna Slater on your wall, haven't you?" asked Jaimini.

"Yes."

"Well, I think you need to take it down. It's probably the last thing you look at before you go to sleep, and that's what's making you dream about her."

"But why should I dream about the bomb and everything? Ugh!" I shuddered at the memory.

"We often dream about our fears," said Fen. "Do you have a subconscious fear that you won't be able to play the piano because of something that you can't control?"

"I don't think so," I said slowly. "I mean, I know I worry about absolutely everything, but funnily enough I don't think that *is* one of my fears."

"But if it's subconscious, it may be so deep that nothing except the power of this horrific nightmare will bring it to the surface," breathed Luce in a husky voice, as she slowly stood up and stared dramatically into the middle distance with a strange look in her eyes.

"Thank you, Psychoanalyst Edmunson," said Jaimini, yanking Luce back down again, which made the rest of us laugh. Andy just smiled. She was, as usual, the only one not to have spoken.

"What do you think, Andy?" I asked her.

"I think the brain is amazingly complex," she replied. We all looked at her, waiting for her to go on, but she'd finished. The bell rang and up we got.

"Going to the café after school?" Luce asked anyone who might feel like answering.

"I'm on duty," said Tash.

"I'll go," said Fen.

In the end we all agreed to go, which we often did after school. It's a great place to meet for a drink and a chat, even if you're not actually working there. Sometimes we have clubs or practices, or in my case music lessons, after school, so it's not always possible for all of us to go to the café.

I was looking forward to it today, though, because my timetable for the rest of the day was so awful. I don't particularly like games because I'm not much good at it, and I hate science. There was only one lesson that I was looking forward to, and that was music.

Our music teacher is called Mrs Merle. She's very popular because she's kind and fair. The music teacher before her, Miss Farrant, was a real tyrant but it turned out that she had cancer and she couldn't help being so horrible all the time. She's left now and I'm good friends with her. I go to visit her regularly.

As I pushed open the door to the music room I

was thinking about Miss Farrant. I'd learnt a new piece on my violin and I was dying to play it to her, because I knew it would be just her kind of music. I made a resolution then and there to go and see her after school. Maybe I'd buy one of Kevin's famous cakes at the café and take that to Miss Farrant. Kevin is the chef at the café, by the way.

Fen, Tash and Andy do music at the same time as me, but I'd gone on ahead because I was worrying about being late. I got quite a shock when I went into the classroom because there was no sign of Mrs Merle. In her place at the front stood a rather stern-faced man.

"Yes, yes, come in," he told me, rather impatiently. "Your music teacher's away for a while."

He'd given me no more than a very quick glance before returning to his books and paper on the desk at the front. I got the impression he wasn't really prepared. He seemed very flustered. By this time the rest of the class were filtering in, including my friends, who I'd saved places for.

"Who's he?" Andy whispered as she sat down.

"Mrs Merle's away. He must be a supply teacher."

The rest of the class were all talking in whispers. It's always like this when there's a new teacher. It takes a few minutes to size them up. I could hear a bit of sniggering at the back of the class. Obviously the boys who always sat at the back in music had already made up their minds about our replacement music teacher.

"Right. Quiet."

Still he didn't really look at us. Not properly anyway. He just turned to the board and wrote Mr Grote in large letters. Of course, that caused louder sniggers from the back, and then I realized that Robert Taylor was trying out his "torch-pen torture".

Robert Taylor is a bit of a comic. If I was more laid-back, I'd really find him funny, but I'm not, so I just worry whenever he starts winding teachers up. His pen has got the most minute torch in the end of it. It's like the finest thread of light you could imagine. Robert is very clever at throwing this wispy beam wherever he wants, just by holding the pen and directing the beam very quickly and accurately. He once threw it all round my face and it took me ages to work out what it was, because you feel as though there's a little insect or something flying about just near your head, and then something seems to go in your eyes and you find yourself batting it away with your hand because you just can't work out what's going on.

I watched Mr Grote flapping his hand about near his face and looking irritated and confused, then dodging his head this way and that, while the boys at the back were presumably aching with the strain of stifling their laughter. Fen was enjoying it, too, I could tell, but I think Tash was beginning to feel uncomfortable, as I was. I wished Robert would stop. He'd done it for long enough and we didn't know what Mr Grote was like. If he was one of those teachers who run on a very short fuse, Robert could be in big trouble. On the other hand, *no* teacher had ever worked out Robert's clever little game, and though a few teachers had got cross and said things like, "Look, I know that someone is having a practical joke here, and I'm warning whoever it is that if it doesn't stop, they'll be in deep trouble," Robert never did get into deep trouble.

Andy's face wore an expression that I recognized. I'd once asked Dad what it's called when you can't tell what another person is thinking by the expression on their face. Dad said that the word was *inscrutable*. That was how Andy was looking. Inscrutable.

"I suggest that whoever is responsible for this laser beam flying about the room owns up now, if he or she doesn't want to get the rest of the class into trouble."

There was a silence, because no one had expected Mr Grote to work out that the irritating thing was actually a beam of light, and certainly no other teacher had ever been so clever as to smoke out the culprit by threatening trouble for the rest of the class like this.

Tash's face, which is always pale, went white, and I knew exactly what she was thinking. She was worried in case Mr Grote suddenly sprang a detention on the whole class, because that would mean that she'd be late for work at the café.

"I shall find out and I shall confiscate the article unless the person responsible owns up first."

Without thinking, I turned round to Robert Taylor because I felt sure he would admit then that it had been him. The moment I'd done it I could have died because I knew I'd given the game away. Facing the front again I could feel a blush covering my whole face. Mr Grote was staring at me, but then he transferred his gaze to the back of the room and a slow, gloating smile appeared on his face.

It seemed an eternity but it probably only took him about five seconds to get to the back of the class. This time everybody *but* me turned round to see what would happen.

"He knows," whispered Fen, and then I did turn round, to see Mr Grote holding out his hand to Robert Taylor, palm up.

"What?" asked Robert in a hurt voice, as though he'd been unfairly picked on.

"Hand it over … and please don't say 'what' again, because you know exactly what I mean."

"I … don't, actually," said Robert, sounding much less sure of himself. His eyes flashed at me, and I knew at that moment that one of two things would happen. Either *I* would be in trouble with Robert, for giving away that he was the guilty one, or Robert himself would be in trouble. I wondered where the torch-pen was. In the desk? In his bag? Up his sleeve?

"Mr Grote?" came Andy's voice into the tense silence. My eyes widened. It wasn't like Andy to get involved in things like this unless she felt very strongly about something or other. In a flash all eyes were on Andy, including Mr Grote's.

"What exactly is the matter with Mrs Merle?" she asked, innocently.

Mr Grote looked as though he'd explode. Red-faced, he turned straight back to Robert, completely ignoring Andy's question. But it was too late, as he probably realized. Andy's clever diversion had given Robert just enough time to get rid of the torch-pen.

"What is your name?" Mr Grote asked Andy as he swung on his heel and strode back to the front.

"Agnès Sorrell."

"And yours?" His eyes were on me.

"Leah Bryan."

"And you at the back?"

"Robert Taylor."

Mr Grote was writing our names down, then he returned to the back of the class and addressed Robert.

"Put your hands on the desk, please."

I held my breath as Robert slowly did as he was told. There was no sign of the pen. I couldn't work it out at all, and judging by the look on his face, neither could Mr Grote.

"I see," he said, closing his eyes and opening them again in a slow, impatient gesture, which made my whole body tense up. "Empty your pockets quickly so that we can get on with the lesson."

It was obvious everyone was really hoping that Robert would take his time, because this was infinitely more gripping than learning music. Robert did as he was asked but there was no torch-pen, only a biro, a rubber band, a key and a charge card. Goodness knows how Robert managed to get rid of the pen so quickly, but it was all thanks to Andy.

"I see," Mr Grote repeated, which was probably the least fitting thing he could have said, because he didn't "see" at all. I don't know how my mind managed to let such a trivial thought come up when I was actually feeling worried sick that Robert would hate me for giving the game away. Mr Grote obviously then decided to abandon the search because he turned suddenly to Andy, and said with great sarcastic emphasis, "Mrs Merle is absent. Why she is absent is none of your business. Now we'll try and do a bit of music, I think."

He started to write loads of notes on the blackboard and, with the drama apparently over, everyone grew very restless. The lesson was fairly quiet after that, though, because nobody else felt like messing with Mr Grote. The moment the bell went we all stood up and I rushed out quickly without waiting for the others because I wanted to avoid Robert Taylor. As I hurried along the corridor to games I wished for the millionth time that I was more like Andy. Everyone respected Andy, even the boys. Especially the boys.

It was a big relief when school finished that day and we were all sitting in the café surrounded by bustle and atmosphere.

"What's new?" asked Jan, with a smile for us all as she served us with banana milk shakes, our latest craze.

"A horrible supply teacher has replaced Mrs Merle, our favourite teacher," Fen told her.

"Oh, dear. Got him for long?"

"Hope not," I mumbled.

"He *must* be bad if Leah doesn't like him!"

With that Jan hurried off at fifty miles per hour as usual. At the till Mark was totting up a customer's bill and Tash was folding napkins. Mark is seventeen and works part time in the café. He spends the rest of his time training in the Martial Arts. He's excellent at throwing people. We've seen him practising but he says he would only ever do it properly as a form of defence. The café was quite full and so we played our favourite game, which is trying to guess what jobs the various customers have got.

"What about that man over there with that woman?" said Luce.

"Probably husband and wife," said Fen.

"Probably not," said Andy.

"Why not?" I asked.

"Body language," answered Andy, in her usual brief way.

"What do you mean, 'body language'?" asked Luce.

"If they *are* married, it's very recent," Jaimini commented, and Andy nodded.

"But how do you know?" asked Luce.

"Because of the way they're looking at each other," Jaimini told her.

"Anyway, I reckon he's a doctor," went on Luce, who was obviously bored with Jaimini's theories.

"No, he works in a hotel and he's on holiday," said Fen.

At that point the man asked Tash for the bill.

She went to get it and we couldn't help noticing that he then handed her a tip. She didn't look at how much it was, because Jan had taught us not to do that on any account. We had to wait till the customer was out of the café, then look subtly and privately at the tip before putting it in the tip box, which was divided up amongst everyone who worked at the café at the end of the week.

"Three pounds," said Tash out of the corner of her mouth, eyes bright, as she passed our table a moment later. "He's a manager. He can afford it," she added.

"How do you know he's a manager?" I asked.

"He's got a little badge with it on," said Tash. "Thcy'rc on thcir way back to somc big confcrence or other."

"Oh, well..." sighed Jaimini. "What about that lady over there?"

"Can't see. She's got her back to us," Luce complained.

"That makes it all the more fun," said Fen. "Guess how old she is from the back of her head."

We all eyed her slightly wavy dark hair which didn't show any trace of grey. I tried to see her hands, but I couldn't. She had a straight back and square shoulders. She was sitting quite still.

"Forty," said Luce.

"Yeah, about that," said Andy.

"Forty-five," said Jaimini.

"Thirty," said Fen.

"Thirty-five," I guessed. "Let's get Jan to say how old she thinks she is from looking at her face, and whichever one of us is nearest gets twenty pence from each of the others."

"Leah, I never knew you were such a gambler," said Fen, pretending to be shocked.

We called Jan over and persuaded her against her better judgement to take a good look at the lady when she was at one of the tables facing her.

"I guess she's about forty-eight," she told us on her return. So we all forked out twenty-pence pieces for Jaimini, then moved on to an old lady in the corner of the café.

It was while we were discussing where this old lady might live that something happened to really shock me. The woman who had had her back to us, turned her head at the sound of someone from a table behind laughing loudly. We could clearly see her face when she turned and I just stared at her, mouth open, eyes wide.

"What's up with Leah?" I heard Luce say from somewhere that sounded very far off.

"Leah! What's the matter?" That was Andy shaking my arm.

"It's Anna Slater," I whispered, my eyes never leaving the woman's face.

Chapter 2

"Are you sure, Leah?" Andy asked me.

"Course I'm sure. I've got her poster on my wall. I've seen another picture of her in a magazine as well."

"But what would she be doing in Cableden?" asked Jaimini.

"I don't know. Maybe she's on holiday."

"Look. Someone's coming to join her," said Fen.

Sure enough, a tall, good-looking man of about twenty-five was heading straight for Anna Slater's table. He bent down and kissed Anna on the cheek. I began to feel even more sure I was right, and with this certainty, a great excitement was building up inside me. I wanted to go straight over and ask for her autograph, but I decided that this would be rather a babyish thing to do.

"Look, she's drumming her fingers on the

table," remarked Luce. "That's what *you* do, Leah. That proves she's a musician. It *is* her!"

I noticed Andy and Jaimini roll their eyes at each other, so they obviously didn't think much of Luce's little observation.

"It's like you're psychic or something," Fen said. "I mean, don't you think it's an incredible coincidence that you keep dreaming about Anna Slater, and then Anna Slater suddenly appears in our café?"

"Leah, you're psychic," breathed Luce, eyes bright. "Let's test you out. What mark am I going to get for tonight's geography homework?"

"Don't be ridiculous," said Fen. "Psychic people don't know absolutely everything that's going to happen. If they did, their lives would be unbearable."

"Anyway, why do you want to know about tonight's geography homework?" said Jaimini. "I would have thought there were tons of other things you'd rather know than that."

"Well, the thing is, if Leah doesn't reckon I'm going to get a very good mark, I won't bother to do it, but if she thinks it's going to be a brilliant mark, I'd better go home and get on with it."

"You're mad!" Andy told Luce, shaking her head and eyeing Luce as though she was beyond help.

"I once read that Anna Slater lives with

someone quite a bit younger than her," I said, changing the subject.

"And you think that's *him*?" asked Luce, jerking her head rather unsubtly towards the man.

I nodded.

"Go and get her autograph. *I* would," said Luce.

"I don't want to," I said simply, and that was that.

A few minutes later Fen said, "Oh well, I've got to go," so we all decided to leave. The others had waved to Tash across the café and were at the door. I took my time, because although I didn't want to ask for Anna Slater's autograph, I *did* want her to notice me, so I gave her a huge smile as I walked past her table. She smiled back but looked as though she couldn't believe I was actually smiling at *her*. I made it quite clear that I was, by saying "hello". She didn't reply, but I didn't mind. I followed the others out of the café, and all the way home I savoured the moment when she'd smiled back at me.

I could just imagine her and her partner talking about me after I'd gone out. I thought their conversation might have gone something like this:

"That girl obviously recognized you, Anna."

"Yes, I couldn't believe at first that she was actually smiling at *me*."

"Well, you *are* quite famous, after all."

"Yes, but only in musical circles."

"She must be very interested in music, then. I wonder what she plays."

After that I pictured them having a guessing game about what instruments I played. I loved hugging all these thoughts to myself. In fact, I was so wrapped up in them that I'd almost got all the way home before I remembered that I was going to go and visit my old music teacher, Miss Farrant. The trouble was I'd completely forgotten to buy her one of Kevin's cakes, so I decided that I'd leave the visit till the following day. It was Friday the next day, and my turn to work.

I was the first to get home that day and I went straight upstairs to my room to look at my poster and then do some practice. The sight of Anna Slater had really spurred me on. The moment I got my music out, I remembered something very important that had completely slipped my mind. The following evening I was supposed to be playing the violin and the piano at a concert in Limendowling, which is a little town quite near Cableden. It would be a tight squeeze to fit everything in – working at the café, seeing Miss Farrant, then the concert – but there would be just about enough time if I hurried.

The next day at school was pretty uneventful, except for orchestral practice. There are about twenty of us in the school orchestra, and I'm the leader. We're all very keen, because Mrs Merle makes it interesting and good fun. She always chooses music that we like. Mr Grote used all the same music and seemed very good at conducting. Everything was going fine until he suddenly said, "I just want to try something out. Leah, can you swap places with David Laws, please?"

I could feel the blood running from my face because I was so worried. The thing is, it's an honour to be chosen as the leader of the orchestra and unless you've done something really bad, or someone suddenly dramatically overtakes you, you remain as leader until you leave. I couldn't work out why David Laws was taking my place, and I felt very shaky as I got up to swap places with him. Until this moment I had been very confident that I was quite far ahead of him as far as the violin goes, but now my confidence was shaken. He looked as surprised as I felt and the rest of the orchestra seemed shocked and still.

Sitting one row behind my usual position, I tried to concentrate on the rest of the practice, but I couldn't. I was too upset. I kept on telling myself that David was only taking my place for a few minutes, and that any second now Mr Grote would swap us back. But when the bell went for the beginning of afternoon school I was still sitting in the second row feeling really depressed.

I deliberately took as long as I could to pack

away my violin and music, so that I'd be left on my own in the hall with Mr Grote, giving him the chance to explain that next time everything would be back to normal. But when I looked up a few minutes later I saw that Mr Grote had gone out, too, and I was on my own in the hall. I could have cried, but I didn't.

On the way down to the café after school I told Andy what had happened. She frowned but didn't say anything.

"Can you think of any reason why Mr Grote doesn't want me as the leader any more?" I eventually asked her when she still wasn't saying anything.

"The only reason I can think of is that he can't be much of a musician, because even *I* can tell that David Laws has got the ability of a tapeworm compared to you."

I couldn't help smiling at Andy's words, and made a mental note to remember what she'd said whenever I was feeling depressed. We parted at the café and I went in through the back door to the kitchen while she went in through the front door. The others were not far behind.

"Is that smile for me?" Kevin asked me as I closed the door behind me and went to get an apron out of the drawer.

I was about to say that I was smiling at something that Andy had said but I thought that sounded a bit cruel to Kevin, so I just said, "Yes."

Kevin is twenty-one, small, wiry and very fit. He's also a really nice man, and one of very few words. Although he doesn't say much, and he doesn't appear to be taking any notice of anything except his cooking, he has an amazing knack of knowing exactly what's going on. He even seemed to know what was going on inside my head, if his next question was anything to go by.

"Still the leading musical light at Cableden Comp, are you?"

I didn't feel like talking about what had happened in orchestra, so I just smiled and Kevin didn't say any more about it after that. When I mentioned that I was going to take a cake to Miss Farrant, he insisted that I could take one out of the freezer and that I shouldn't pay anything for it.

"It'll be just ready for eating this evening if you take it out now," he said. "She'll love it," he added. "No one can resist my Mississippi Mud Mousse."

"I thought it was 'Pie'."

"Nope. Mousse."

Well, I said Kevin was a man of few words, didn't I!

I didn't have to go into the café for another twenty minutes and when I did, I got a shock because Anna Slater was there again with the same man. They were drinking tea and eating scones and I kept praying that they'd both want more of something so that *I* could be the one to serve them. I still wouldn't ask for her autograph but I'd say something to show I knew who she was. That would strike her as very mature, I felt sure. I'd say something like, "I suppose even the best violinists have days off."

I was so pleased with this line that I kept on repeating it to myself to make sure that I wouldn't forget it when it came to saying it.

"Do you want me to get her autograph for you?" asked Luce, swinging back in her chair as I went past their table.

"No," I frowned.

"What about *his*?" she persisted.

"He's not even famous," I whispered back.

"Shame," said Luce, her head on one side. "Still, I suppose it's better to be good-looking than famous."

Every thirty seconds I found my eyes straying over to Anna Slater's table in the hope that she or the man might be about to attract my attention for some more tea, but they never did, and I was having to try to think of a reason why I might just talk to them without them ordering anything else. The only thing I could think of was to ask them if everything was all right, like Jan had done the previous day. I was on the point of going over and making this pleasant enquiry when, miracle of miracles, I realized the man was trying to catch my eye.

Like some kind of jet-propelled, ground-covering firework, I shot over to their table with a massive grin on my face and stood with my pad and pencil at the ready.

"Could we have the bill, please?" asked the man.

"Oh … yes, of course." I felt sad that they would be gone shortly, because the chances of their coming into the café a third time were very small. Right, I would have to say my carefully prepared line, and see what Anna said to that.

I put their bill face down on the table and launched in with another of my big, warm smiles. "I suppose even the best violinists have days off."

Immediately something in the atmosphere went very cold. I had no idea what on earth I'd said wrong. A quick glance to my left told me that all the others had their eyes on me, and all I could think was that something awful was happening and I wished everyone would go away so that this terrible thing could happen to me without an audience. Anna Slater's face had masked over with a hard look, and she had lowered her eyes.

The man looked a mixture of embarrassed and irritated. He coughed and muttered, "Thank you for the bill," then, as I was still standing there like a statue, he added a more forceful "*Thank you*," and I scuttled away with red cheeks and a pounding heart. It wasn't enough to go over to the counter. I needed to get right away, so I went into the kitchen, and then, feeling that even this wasn't far enough away, I opened the back door and went outside, taking great gulps of fresh air and praying that Kevin wouldn't follow me out to see what was the matter. I should have known he wouldn't. Kevin never interferes unless he's asked to.

It was Luce who came to find me outside with the words, "You were wrong, Lee. That's not Anna Slater, it's someone called Elizabeth Driscoll, and the man's her son. I asked Becky."

Becky also works part-time at the café. None of us have much in common with her, though it's true she seems to know an awful lot of the customers.

"But why...?"

I was about to ask her if Becky knew how come it was so terrible to say what I'd said, when I suddenly realized that maybe Luce hadn't even heard me say it. And if *she* hadn't heard, maybe the others hadn't either, so at least I wouldn't have to be embarrassed for ever.

"Why what?"

"Doesn't matter."

"Were you going to ask why they both went all

quiet on you when you said something about famous violinists?"

So she *had* heard. I nodded, as a great wave of depression covered me and seeped all through me from my head to my toes.

"No idea. Neither have the others and neither has Jan or Becky, but we all agree you must have dropped an awful clanger to have made them both react like they did."

Things were going from bad to worse. I had "dropped an awful clanger" and the others had witnessed it. Then, just to put the icing on the cake, Jan and Becky knew as well. I felt like curling up and dying. Half of me wanted to know what was so bad, but the other half was scared to find out.

"Anyway, they've gone now, so the coast is clear if you want to go back into the café," Luce went on blithely. She obviously had no idea at all how bad I was feeling. "Oh, and the others all say 'bye' and 'have a nice weekend' and 'play well at the concert tonight'."

"Thanks."

For nothing. I felt drained. I stayed in the kitchen for ages, washing up at about one mile per hour until Jan came in and gently told me that I ought to work a little more quickly. I could tell Jan wasn't too happy, which only made me feel even worse.

About ten minutes later I ventured back into the café to find that only Luce and Jaimini had gone after all. The others were still sitting there. Andy mouthed "You OK?" at me and I nodded, but it was only a very small nod and I don't think she believed me.

It was a relief to see that the man and woman had gone but just looking at their table, which was still empty, made me feel a fool. How could I have possibly got that woman mixed up with Anna Slater? Now I tried to visualize Anna Slater's face on my poster, she didn't look a bit like this woman. But what was wrong with what I'd said? Why was it so terrible? I could have understood it if they thought I was slightly loopy because of coming out with something that had nothing to do with this Elizabeth Driscoll person, but surely they'd realize I'd got her mixed up with someone else, wouldn't they? And yet the way they'd both reacted, you'd think I'd accused her of being a mass murderer or something.

"Leah! What on earth are you doing?" Jan's voice interrupted my thoughts.

I jumped, and that made matters worse. You see, I'd been so deep in thought that I'd poured sugar into a salt cellar at the counter, then when Jan had startled me I'd tipped the bag of sugar a bit too much and sent a sugar waterfall on to the floor.

"Sorry! Oh, sorry, Jan! I was miles away."

"So I gather," said Jan, through tight lips. "Clear it up quickly and try to get your mind back on your work, Leah."

I blushed and glanced over to see if the others had been watching. They were all pretending to be deep in conversation, but I could tell they'd seen what had happened. I bet they thought I was totally stupid. And no wonder. I *was* stupid, *and* clumsy.

About a minute later they went, which proved that I was right. They just about managed to wave to me when they got to the door, but it was obvious they couldn't get away quickly enough. I spent the whole of the rest of my duty getting things wrong and making Jan more and more cross. I wrote down two orders incorrectly and then delivered the wrong order to the wrong table.

Jan's lips seemed to get thinner and thinner the crosser she got, and she also moved more and more quickly, so that by almost six o'clock when it was nearly time for me to go she was whizzing round the café at about a hundred miles per hour.

"Just polish the tables and then you'd better go, Leah," she told me rather curtly.

It was when I was spraying my third table that Jan suddenly grabbed the polish out of my hand, and said, "Leah! What *is* the matter with you?

This is air freshener, not furniture polish!"

At that point I almost burst into tears, which made me feel even worse because it was so babyish for a girl of my age to feel like crying over something like this. I bit my lip and blinked my eyes a lot before whispering, "Sorry. I'll do them all again."

"Just go, Leah," said Jan, making it quite clear that she'd had absolutely enough of me, so I put my apron away, picked up my school bag and went. I'd got one of Kevin's cakes in my bag, but I didn't think I had the energy to visit Miss Farrant now. She wouldn't appreciate a visit from a miserable, pathetic girl anyway. It would be better to go and see her another time when I was feeling better; if I *ever* felt better again.

On the other hand I didn't want to go straight home and I definitely didn't feel like playing in a stupid concert. I obviously wasn't as good at playing the violin as everybody thought I was. Come to think of it, not everybody *did* think I was. In fact, I could count the number of people who thought I was any good on one hand ... my violin teacher, my mum, my dad, Miss Farrant and Mrs Merle.

You couldn't really count Mum and Dad, either, because they were prejudiced, so that left only three people. Mrs Merle had never been anything except full of compliments and kindness for me and my playing, and suddenly it seemed very important to go and see her. I knew she could make me feel better. She was one of the nicest people I knew. So I turned and began to walk quickly in the other direction. I'd give the cake to Mrs Merle to make up for the fact that I was disturbing her when she was officially away from school, then I'd go and visit Miss Farrant another day. I began to feel better instantly, and broke into a run, which turned straight back into a walk, followed by a very slow, reluctant walk because it suddenly occurred to me that I shouldn't be doing this.

Mrs Merle was absent from school, and Mr Grote had been fairly cagey about why she was away. She might not even be ill. Maybe she was pregnant! No, she wouldn't be having time off school before the baby even showed, would she? What I was desperately hoping was that she'd turn out to be just a little bit ill, but definitely not ill enough to hate the thought of visitors or anything.

My footsteps quickened again and by the time I got to her house, I'd convinced myself that she'd had twenty-four-hour flu and she was now completely over it, and looking forward to coming back to school after the weekend. I'd only ever been to Mrs Merle's house once before, to practise a piece for a school assembly. She had been accompanying me on the piano and we hadn't had time to practise it in school.

I rang the bell and waited, but as the seconds went by I began to get the horribly depressing feeling that she wasn't there. But she *must* be there. She was ill. I pressed the bell harder as though this would make a difference, then I stood back a bit and looked up at the upstairs window to see if she was beckoning to me to go round the back or anything.

The back! Of course! She was in bed so she didn't want to come down and answer the door. I went through the side gate, round to the back, and up the three steps to the door. I knocked gently in case she happened to be in the kitchen, but no one answered. The last time I'd been to Mrs Merle's house she'd been expecting me but, even so, she hadn't answered my knock, and although I'd worried that I was being too forward, I'd opened the back door and called out from the kitchen. She'd come smiling and rushing through from the hall and said she was sorry, she hadn't heard me. Maybe that's what I should do now. I turned the handle and sure enough, the door opened.

"Mrs Merle, hello," I called in a sing-songy voice, then when she still didn't answer I called out two or three more times as I crept through the kitchen and into the hall, hesitating at the bottom of the stairs. "Hello, Mrs Merle, it's me. Leah Bryan. I was wondering how you are..."

My eyes strayed to the open sitting-room door. Nobody was in there and the room looked exactly as it had done the last time I'd been to this house. All Mrs Merle's things to do with music were in here. Not just her hi-fi and cassettes and CDs, but her piano and all her sheet music. She had the most beautiful antique music cabinet with a lovely carved metronome on it. I'd particularly admired the metronome when I'd been here the last time. Then there was a very ornate music box, which I knew was extremely precious to Mrs Merle. It had been passed down through her family from her great-grandmother.

Returning to the bottom of the stairs I tried calling one more time, but I knew there would be no answer. The silence in the house seemed too great for there to be anyone there, and I could practically hear my heart beat. Half of me wanted to turn round and get out as quickly as possible, but the other half was hanging on to the slim chance that Mrs Merle was upstairs and she couldn't hear anything because she'd got her Walkman on.

A sudden noise behind me made me swing round in terror. My school bag banged hard against the banister. The noise had come from the kitchen. If there was someone in there, they would definitely know that they were not alone in the house. My bag had really clonked hard against the banister, and my heart felt as though it was in my throat.

Maybe Mrs Merle was lying upstairs in bed, while a burglar was in her kitchen. I felt petrified and didn't know which way to turn, so I just stayed still and wished my heart would quieten down a bit. But instead of calming down, it missed a beat, and the hairs on my arms stood up as the door from the kitchen to the hall began to open. There was nowhere to hide, even if I'd been capable of moving, so I just tensed up and froze as a black and white cat strolled into the hall without a glance in my direction, then ran lightly upstairs.

Slumping over the banister I waited for my heart to get back to normal, then I forced myself to go back into the kitchen, just to check it *had* been the cat that had made the noise. There certainly didn't appear to be anything different about the kitchen so taking my courage in both hands, I decided to venture upstairs, calling out "Hello … hello, Mrs Merle", all the way. My voice wasn't sing-songy this time because I was so worried about what I was doing, but I just *had* to know if Mrs Merle was all right. I'd never been upstairs in this house before so I'd no idea which was Mrs Merle's bedroom. I didn't even know if there was a Mr Merle. Mrs Merle had certainly never mentioned a husband, so maybe she was divorced. It suddenly occurred to me that I really didn't know very much about my teacher at all, and yet here I was, walking upstairs uninvited in her house, my heart banging against my ribs.

The first thing I noticed from the top of the stairs was that all the doors were wide open. There were three bedrooms and a bathroom. The second thing I noticed was that all three bedrooms were nice and tidy. I knew Mrs Merle was a tidy person because she was so organized about everything, and tidiness and organization go together I always think. There was no need to investigate any further; Mrs Merle was definitely not upstairs.

Suddenly my courage ran out. I felt as though *I* was an intruder, and I just had to get away immediately. I raced downstairs, through the kitchen and out of the back door, only pausing to pull the door firmly shut behind me. Then I set off as fast as I could for home.

Chapter 3

"Leah! Where on earth have you been?" was Mum's greeting as I went in through the back door.

For a moment I couldn't understand why she seemed so stressed, but then I realized. The concert. I'd been so intent on trying to see Mrs Merle that I'd forgotten all about the concert. And the only reason I'd gone to Mrs Merle's in the first place was because of that stupid incident in the café with Elizabeth Driscoll. That was what was responsible for making me do everything wrong, so that Jan and the others thought I was hopeless. I said sorry to Mum without giving any explanation, then rushed upstairs to get ready as quickly as I could.

The first thing I saw on entering my bedroom was the poster of Anna Slater. I stopped and stared hard at it. For the second time that day I decided I must be going round the bend or something, because Elizabeth Driscoll looked about as much like Anna Slater as I looked like Mary Poppins. I wanted to blame everything on Elizabeth Driscoll with her nasty cold expression and her horrible insensitive attitude, but in my heart I knew I couldn't, because the blame lay with me.

I'd definitely said something wrong. Even Luce thought that I'd dropped a huge clanger. Andy probably thought I was really pathetic, and Jan knew for sure that I was. She'd witnessed my clumsy attempts at being a waitress. I wouldn't be surprised if she told Fen to try and get someone else to take my place, just like Mr Grote had done. He'd got David Laws to take my place as leader of the orchestra. I couldn't do anything properly any more.

All the time I'd been having these thoughts, my eyes hadn't left the poster of Anna Slater. She was staring right back at me in a very knowing way. I shivered and shook my head two or three times to try and get rid of the picture of those eyes, but it was no good. I couldn't. It was as though she'd got me under her spell and I couldn't escape.

"Leah, are you ready?"

Mum was sounding really stressed by now so I changed faster than I ever had before into my black trousers and purple top, then I brushed my hair vigorously for about ten seconds, grabbed my violin and belted downstairs.

The concert was taking place in Limendowling village hall, which is a big, modern building. As Mum, Dad and I crept in we were met at the door by a very anxious-looking Mrs Prentice, my violin teacher.

"So sorry, Mrs Prentice. Leah was late back from the café." Mum had got her you-know-what-teenagers-are-like look on her face, but Mrs Prentice wasn't interested in why I was late, she just wanted to get me into "concert mode" as quickly as possible.

"You look pale, Leah. Are you all right?" she asked me as we took our places in the audience.

"Nerves," I answered, which was an understatement. The truth was I felt sick. I've always suffered from terrible nerves whenever I've had to play for a concert, exam or anything. I can't help it. But today seemed even worse because I knew I wasn't as good as I used to be. If only Mrs Merle had been in, she would have reassured me that I could still play. Maybe Mrs Prentice would do the same. I began to think how I could get on to the subject. The audience was still talking quietly but I knew that at any moment the concert would begin. I was the third item in the programme.

"We've got a new music teacher at school," I whispered to Mrs Prentice.

"That's nice," she said, but I knew she wasn't

really paying attention. Her eyes were darting about all over the room.

"He's dropped me as leader of the orchestra."

"Ssh. They're starting."

I had been hoping for a load of sympathy, but she hadn't even heard me. My words had sounded very loud to me, though. I felt as though they were still there, hanging up in that hall for everyone to see and laugh at.

He's dropped me as leader of the orchestra.

Someone was walking to the front to go up on the stage. A man. I sighed deeply because I really did not feel like being here in this room. Playing the violin was the very last thing I wanted to do, and the next-to-last thing was to listen to anyone else playing a musical instrument. The man was obviously a pianist. He was slowly sitting down at the piano. His page turner was taking his place in a chair at his side. I gasped. It was Mr Grote and David Laws. I'd known there was something familiar about them, I was just being amazingly slow to click on.

Now I felt more uncomfortable than ever. I leaned over to Mrs Prentice and whispered, "That's him – the new music teacher."

"Gregory Grote?"

"Is that his name, Gregory?"

She nodded and sat up a bit straighter, as though it was more important to really listen, now she knew it was my music teacher. He began to play and I tried to concentrate, but I just kept going over and over in my mind how he'd got me to swap places with David Laws, and now here was David Laws again, like some kind of devoted disciple.

I watched David staring at the music, and noticed something I'd never noticed before. He'd got a twitch. Every so often his head would move just a fraction. It was definitely a twitch. Fancy never having noticed that before… Although I supposed it wasn't that surprising because I'd never really noticed anything about David Laws, except that he was usually on his own, not with friends, and that he'd got sandy-coloured hair and a head that seemed somehow too big for his body. I dragged my eyes away from David and looked at Mr Grote. He was a really good pianist. There was no doubt about it.

The piece he was playing was a very long one by Debussy. Every time David leaned forward to turn the page, I thought he was going to be too late because it took him so long. I began to wonder if there was something wrong with his hand, unless Mr Grote had particularly told him to turn the pages slowly, so I watched very closely at the next page turn, and noticed that his hand was actually trembling. Maybe he was nervous about being on show like that.

Mr Grote's playing was getting better and better. He must have huge hands to manage all those big stretchy passages, but there wasn't a single stumble and he was reaching the climax of the piece. It was so brilliant that for a moment I forgot all about my own problems and just lost myself in his lovely music. Then, bang!

The whole audience jumped because David had dropped the music in the middle of turning the page, and it had fallen on to Mr Grote's hands. An awful wave of tension ran over the audience as the pages of music rustled into the silence.

I wondered how Mr Grote would react. It must have really affected him badly to have been interrupted so suddenly like that. How could he possibly continue? The spell had been broken; the audience was restless. I wondered what he'd do, but he just patted David awkwardly on the shoulder and gave him a smile – as if to reassure him that it wasn't his fault, when of course it *was* really – then he carried on from where he'd left off, but the audience wasn't the same after. Their attention had gone. So had mine. My nice dreamy state had evaporated, and the nervous tension was back with a vengeance. More than ever now, I did *not* want to play.

Mr Grote's presence just made me even more nervous. He'd be watching me, and deciding whether or not to have me back as the leader of the orchestra. The thought of that was guaranteed to make me play badly, and that would let Mrs Prentice down. A local musician who liked setting up musical events had written to her, along with all the other local instrumental teachers, to see if any of them had any pupils who were grade six or higher and would be able to play in the concert. Mrs Prentice had been so pleased and proud to put my name forward. I'd never before played at a concert organized by this person, though I *had* played in Limendowling village hall before.

The audience clapped like mad when Mr Grote's piece had finished and I watched David clapping. His hands seemed completely normal, and the twitch appeared to have gone, too. Maybe I'd imagined that there was something wrong with his hand, and maybe he only twitched when he was concentrating. It was all very puzzling. Or perhaps it was self-consciousness that made him look so awkward. There was one more player to come before me. It was a flautist. As I listened to the flute playing I had a thought. Perhaps it was fate that I'd been given this perfect opportunity to show Mr Grote that I *could* play the violin. If I played my very, very best, surely he'd let me be the leader of the orchestra again.

This thought really fired me up, and although

I was nervous, I was trying like mad to be like Fen would have been in this situation – ambitious and single-minded.

"Don't hurt yourself," Mum whispered, putting her hand over mine for a moment.

I wondered what on earth she meant, then I realized I'd been pressing my right-hand thumbnail into my left palm, and I hadn't even noticed how hard I'd been doing it. There was a definite red mark on my left palm. I began to drum my fingers on my legs and to stretch them to warm them up. Mrs Prentice was accompanying me on the piano and I was glad because that meant that the audience had two people to look at. I hated it when they were totally focused on me.

The flute piece came to an end and my heart started its usual drum solo that it did every time just before I had to go up on a stage. I didn't dare look at the audience because I didn't want to have to say hello to Mr Grote, so I kept my eyes down, apart from looking at Mrs Prentice when I'd tuned up and was ready to start.

Considering I felt such a wreck, I think I played the first two pages of the piece really well, probably better than I'd ever played them before, in fact. Good. Now *surely* Mr Grote would change his mind and let me be the leader of the orchestra again. I was just in the middle of a slow, soft, descending scale passage when I noticed a tiny movement out of the corner of my eye. Stupidly I let my eyes stray just for a second from my music, and saw to my horror that Mr Grote was coming through the door. He was being very discreet and stayed just inside the door.

If it had been anyone else it wouldn't have put me off, but of course it did, because I had thought that Mr Grote was already in the room listening to me. I couldn't believe that he'd missed all that playing that had gone so well. My bow promptly slipped and I played two horribly wrong notes, which completely fazed me so that my bow started shaking. Mrs Prentice had noticed. I could feel her eyes boring into me.

Oh, why did I always have to *feel* everything so much? Why couldn't I be like Luce and let things wash over me? Mistake after mistake fell from my violin and my face grew hotter and hotter. Mr Grote was getting the benefit of the worst violin playing I'd ever done. It was all so unfair. It hardly seemed worth trying to get it back together because I was practically at the end of the piece and the damage was done.

When I'd finished, the audience really clapped loudly, but that only made me blush all the more because they clearly just felt sorry for me. They were giving me tons of encouragement, like you would for a little kid who'd got up to say a poem then stuttered and stammered hopelessly through it. The clapping made me more depressed than ever because I'm not a little kid. I wanted to call out, "*Look I* can *play this piece properly, you know. I only messed it up because of* him *turning up in the middle.*"

I didn't dare look at the audience as I made my way back to my place. I didn't even look at Mum and Dad, and thank goodness they didn't say a word. There were two more items before the interval, a choir and a quartet. I couldn't enjoy them at all. I found myself looking round the audience to see if there was anyone else there that I knew, but as far as I could see without actually turning my head too obviously, there wasn't, thank goodness. I tried to comfort myself with this. At least I'd only made a fool of myself in front of David Laws and Mr Grote.

My eyes swivelled as far to the right as they could and I noticed to my horror that the man who had been with Elizabeth Driscoll in the café was sitting at the end of the very front row. Maybe he had some kind of psychic power or maybe it was a coincidence, but he suddenly turned his head and looked straight at me. Immediately I stared hard at the quartet on the stage, but for a split second our eyes had met and in that second I could tell he wanted to say something. I did not like that look in his eyes. He probably wanted to tell me off. I decided that I'd work very hard on persuading Mum that we ought to go in the interval. I would plead homework. That would be the best excuse.

As quietly as I could I leaned down and picked up my music from the floor, then mouthed "pencil" at Mrs Prentice. Like a lot of musicians she always carried a pencil around with her, and sure enough she produced one from her pocket and handed it to me. On the back of my music I wrote, *Got tons of homework. Can we go in the interval?* I slipped the music across to Mum's lap.

Mum read the note and gave me a frown, so I raised my eyebrows and she passed the note across to Dad's lap. Dad read it, and leaning across Mum, gave me the same sort of frown that Mum had done. I could tell that Dad didn't mind whether we went or not. The frown was just one of his absent-minded little things that he often did. He's such a lovely dad. I gave him one of my best pleading looks, and he whispered something to Mum, who then gave me a curt little nod before transferring her gaze extra intently to the quartet, as though she ought to get the very most she could out of this item because it was going to be the last.

I heaved a big sigh of relief inside myself. So far so good. Good old Dad. Now I just had to work out what would be the fastest possible way to get out before the sinister-looking man could get me.

The quartet had finished and the audience were clapping. I risked a glance over to the far end of the front row and once again the man was looking at me. This was getting too much. The moment the clapping showed any sign of beginning to fade, I said to Mum, "I'll be outside. I feel sick." Then I said more or less the same thing to Mrs Prentice, before getting up, clambering over the rest of my row and diving out of the door. Our car was parked at the far end of the car park, so I dashed straight over to it and crouched down behind it, out of sight of the village hall. My heart was beating violently again and I wondered if this was how escaped criminals felt.

I could hear footsteps and voices approaching. *Please let it be Mum and Dad*... It was.

"Whatever are you doing down there, Leah?" asked Mum, coming round to the passenger side. "It's all right, Stuart, she's here."

"I felt kind of faint, but I'm a bit better now," I answered, sliding into the car straight from my crouched position so that my head wouldn't show over the top of the car, in case we were being watched.

"What do you think went wrong?" Mum asked me carefully when we were driving along.

"Our new music teacher was there and it put me off," I told her, which was more or less the truth.

Mum turned round and gave me a sympathetic look but made no further comment and I was glad because I didn't want to talk about it any more. I wanted Monday to come, because I was playing in assembly. It had been arranged ages ago. There was me on my violin and two other girls on their recorders. I was determined to play well so that Mr Grote would see that I didn't always play as badly as he'd just heard me play that evening; then I'd get my job back as leader of the orchestra. On the other hand I was feeling really sorry for David Laws, now I'd seen what an odd sort of boy he was. It was obvious why he was never with any friends. I knew what boys could be like, and someone like David Laws would come in for an awful lot of jokes and absolutely no sympathy. All the same I mustn't get too soft. I wanted my place as leader of the orchestra back.

That night I lay in bed and tried my very hardest not to worry about things. I went through my worries one at a time to see if I could get rid of them so that I could go to sleep.

One: I would tell my friends the next day all about Mr Grote and David, and about my playing going all wrong, and they would be really sympathetic which would take their minds off how stupid I'd been in the café. Two: I would apologize to Jan and she would instantly forgive me, saying something like, "Don't worry, we all have off days."

Three: I would go back to Mrs Merle's and confess that I'd been inside her house, and she would say she didn't mind; then I'd tell her all about Mr Grote and David Laws, and she would tell me not to worry because she was coming back on Monday and everything would be back to normal. Four: Jan would mention casually that Elizabeth Driscoll and her son had emigrated to Australia.

The solution to worry number four was rather far-fetched, I knew, but at least I'd sorted out three of my four problems, and I found myself drifting off to sleep.

When I woke up I was sweating. I sat bolt upright in bed and waited for the horrible banal little nursery tune that was penetrating my skull to go away. Staring into the darkness I could still see Anna Slater playing her violin and my own eyes staring out of an ashen face. I snapped the bedside light on and took deep breaths. I'd had that awful nightmare again. Leaping out of bed, I pulled down the poster of Anna Slater, ripping it as I did so. "There," I said, feeling anger mingling in with my terror. Then I sat at my desk and drew silly little cartoon animals to get rid of the memory of the dream. Not until every last shred of dream had disappeared did I get back into bed and switch off the light.

The next day was Saturday and I didn't wake up till quite late.

"Andy phoned," said Kim, as I sat down at the kitchen table with a bowl of cereal.

"Yeah?"

"She's coming round. Is that OK?"

I nodded, feeling happy. Already the first of my worries was about to be cleared up. "When?"

"Five minutes."

Andy and I sat in my room and she immediately noticed the torn and screwed-up poster of Anna Slater on the floor at the end of my bed.

"What's that doing there?" she asked.

"I had that nightmare again. It was awful, so I ripped down the poster. I kind of thought that might help."

"Spooky," said Andy. "Let's have a look at her." She straightened out the poster and tilted her head to one side as she studied it.

"She does look a bit like that woman in the café actually, doesn't she?"

I felt so happy that Andy didn't think I was a complete idiot after all. "All the same I wish I'd never said anything to Elizabeth Driscoll or whatever her name is."

"I should forget about it if I were you. You'll probably never see her again."

So I told Andy all about the concert and she was really sympathetic. She still reckoned that Elizabeth Driscoll's son wasn't worth worrying about, so next I told her about Mrs Merle. I could tell she was much more interested in this story.

"Are you sure there was no one there? I mean, has she got a big garden? Might she have been down at the bottom of it?"

"No, it's only small. I would have seen her if she'd been anywhere around."

"What about a shed or a garage?"

"No, there isn't a shed. And the garage doors were shut. I doubt she would have been in there."

"It's just that it doesn't seem like Mrs Merle to be so forgetful as to leave her house unlocked like that."

Andy was right, and although I'd had the very same thought at the time, I hadn't considered it since. I waited to see if Andy had any ideas, but she didn't say any more. I guessed she'd probably think about it during the day.

"Anyway, the reason I came round was to tell you that Tash's whole family are out tonight and Tash is having a sleep-over. We're all invited. Can you come?"

"Yes, I think so. I'll have to check with Mum."

We agreed to meet up in the café in the afternoon, then all go on to Tash's house from there. It was Fen's turn to work. I had spent ages thinking about it, and finally decided to go to Mrs Merle's beforehand, so straight after lunch I set off and crossed my fingers all the way that she would be there.

As I approached the house a sinking feeling began to come over me and sure enough, when I rang the bell there was no reply. I rang it one more time to make sure, then went round to the back. I was praying that the back door would be locked because I knew I'd never have the guts to go in through the door again. It *was* locked, and though I was relieved in one way, I felt very down because I'd been dying to see Mrs Merle.

I was the last one to turn up at the café. I could see the others through the window as I went in. They immediately beckoned me over and Luce especially was bursting to tell me something.

"That man, Elizabeth Driscoll's son, was here," she told me excitedly. "He came over to our table, and it was obvious he was trying to sound casual, but he wasn't really. He wanted to know where you were."

"What exactly did he say?" I asked, turning to Andy because I knew she'd give me an accurate account of what had happened, whereas Luce's might be jazzed up a bit.

"He said, 'Not got the violinist with you today then?' "

"And what did you lot say?"

"We said you'd be here soon," Luce told me proudly. "Then he looked at his watch as though he was trying to work out whether he'd got enough time to hang around and wait for you."

At that point my eyes flew round the café quickly. "He's not here, is he?" I asked Andy.

"No, don't worry, he went," she told me.

"How did he know you were a violinist?" asked Luce, so I filled them all in on what I'd been telling Andy that morning.

"What do you think he wants you for?" Luce asked me when I'd finished.

"I've no idea, but I didn't like the look in his eyes. I don't want to see him. Not *ever*," I said, rather vehemently.

"You haven't done anything wrong," Tash was quick to point out in her usual kind way.

"So why is he acting as though I've committed a major crime, then?" I asked.

"Oh, no!" said Jaimini, and all our eyes followed her gaze. Coming through the door was the man I never wanted to see again. Without a second thought I got up and bolted into the kitchen, but I knew he'd seen me.

Chapter 4

"What's up, kid?" said Mark.

"Sorry, Mark," I managed to say as I crept round to the other side of him. I'd just hurtled right into him, and yet he was calmly asking me what was wrong. "There's someone in there that I don't want to see," I added, because I felt he deserved an explanation.

My eyes were on the door, and I wouldn't have been surprised to see it open and that awful man appear.

"I'd never have guessed," said Mark with a smile. "Anything I can do?"

"Could you see if there's a tall, dark man in there on his own? He's about twenty-five, I think."

But Mark didn't need to, because Tash came in at that moment to tell me the man had gone. Apparently he'd only hesitated for a moment when he'd seen me go into the kitchen, then he'd just turned and gone out.

"That means he'll be back," I said with a shiver to Tash.

"Look, if someone's bothering you, we can get it sorted out, you know, Leah. What's going on?"

Even Kevin had tuned in by this time. I had Mark on one side of me and Kevin on the other, both looking really concerned.

"No, it's all right. It's my own fault," I said, feeling stupid again.

"All the same..." began Kevin.

"No, honestly Kevin, it's nothing," I insisted, because I just wanted the spotlight off me.

I saw Kevin and Mark exchange looks as Tash and I went back into the café. They were worried, and I could quite see why, but I really did not want anyone else involved with this.

"Right, next time that bloke appears, if I'm with you, I'm going straight up to him to ask him what he wants," Andy told me firmly the moment I sat back down at the table.

"Good for you, Andy," said Fen, who was passing our table at that moment with a cloth in her hand. She'd obviously seen the man, too.

"I think you ought to tell Jan," said Tash.

"No, she'll only ask what exactly I said to them."

"What exactly *did* you say?" asked Jaimini, and

I realized I had to tell them now. It would sound so stupid and they'd all crack up laughing, I was sure.

"Oh, just something about violinists," I said, then desperately tried to think how I could change the conversation without it being too obvious.

"We know that, but *what* exactly?" Luce insisted.

"I can't remember," I lied.

"Yes, you can. Just tell us." Luce wouldn't leave it alone.

"You'll only laugh. It sounds stupid now."

"We won't laugh, we promise," said Tash, but that was typical of Tash and she couldn't speak for the others.

"The thing is, I thought she was Anna Slater, remember?"

"Yes, yes, just tell us," repeated Luce.

"I said, 'I suppose even the best violinists have days off,' " I said.

There was a silence. I looked round. They all wore the same puzzled expression.

"So what's wrong with that?" Jaimini was the first to speak. "OK, so now we know she's not the famous Anna Slater, but so what? It's not offensive or anything."

"No, it's not," Luce agreed, then her eyes suddenly widened and her whole face looked full of something important that she'd just thought of. "I've got it!" she announced.

"What?"

"He's been trying to think where he's seen you before, and now he's remembered. He's seen you in that promotional film you did that time, remember?"

I knew exactly what Luce meant. It was true that I had taken a small part in a promotional film. I liked the idea that someone might have spotted me. It would be wonderful if Luce was right.

"What do you think, Andy?"

"Dunno," replied Andy. She never ever commits herself to anything. Sometimes it's frustrating, but at least when she does give her opinion, there's a pretty high chance that she's going to be right.

"Look who it is," Luce suddenly said. "Hiyah, Rob."

It was Robert Taylor with two of his friends. They all said hello, then sat down at the next table. Robert was showing the other two something or other in a book. Whatever it was, it must have been funny because they couldn't stop laughing. There's something infectious about Robert's laughter. When you hear it you can't help wanting to laugh, too.

After a few minutes, one of the boys, Chris, called out to Jaimini, "What's the French for carpet?"

"I don't know. Ask Andy," said Jaimini.

After Andy had told Chris what he wanted to know, Robert grinned at Jaimini and said, "I thought *you* were supposed to be the brains round here?"

"She is," Luce informed him. "She's my personal homework adviser."

"Oh, right. I don't suppose you can transpose music notes? I haven't the faintest idea how to do that homework Mr Grote set us," said Robert.

"Leah's the musician," Jaimini told him, and that's when Robert deigned to glance at me for the first time. So did the others, only they weren't nice looks. They were completely hostile.

"Sorry, I don't talk to dobbers," Robert said. addressing Jaimini. I could have died. I was so ashamed.

"I never meant to…" I stuttered.

"Never meant to what?" asked Robert coldly. "You mean you never meant to go up to old Gloaty Grote and tell him exactly who it was who was beaming him up the other day?"

"Leah never said a word," Andy quickly defended me.

"How did she do it then? Use sign language?"

I couldn't speak, I was feeling so upset, but Andy was helping me out as usual. "You can't blame Leah for looking round, like she did. She didn't mean to. That's not dobbing."

Fen had obviously seen us talking to Robert and the others and had come over to see what was going on. She caught the general drift.

"Anyway, Andy got you out of trouble," she pointed out to Robert, "and Mr Grote didn't punish you or anything."

"Not much! He only gave me detention and confiscated my pen."

"I never said a word, I swear," I told Robert in a small voice. He looked at me and his eyes narrowed as though he was still deciding whether or not to believe me. "Do you want me to help you with your transposition?" I asked, trying desperately to make amends.

"Forget it," Robert answered me. And with that he turned his back on our table and began more jokey conversation with Chris and the other boy, who I think was called Guy.

"Yeah, forget it," Andy said, turning to me. "It's not your fault, Lee." She looked at the others. "We're all agreed on that, aren't we?"

The others nodded and looked sympathetic, thank goodness.

"I reckon Gloaty Grote saw you looking at Robert, Lee," said Fen, "then cleverly waited till later and pretended to Robert that you'd actually dobbed on him."

"If that's what old Grote did, he needs teaching a lesson," said Andy.

"That is so unfair," agreed Luce.

I didn't say anything, but I felt sure that Fen had guessed right about what had happened.

"Come on, let's go back to my place. Peta will soon cheer you up, Lee."

Peta is Tash's little sister and she's only just three. She's really sweet, though Tash thinks she's quite a pain. Fen was going to join us later, but the rest of us decided to go on ahead. We planned to make a cake for Miss Farrant. I knew she would be delighted to have a visit from five of us, rather than from just me. Also, I sometimes found it quite a strain talking to Miss Farrant on my own, because she was getting weaker and weaker and I never knew whether or not she was in pain and secretly wishing I'd go. With the others there, the conversation would flow much more easily.

Miss Farrant used to be quite a battleaxe as a teacher, but we forgave her when we found out that her cancer affected her mood terribly. She's come to terms with it now and her whole character has really changed. She always says that I was the one who made her "see the light" as she puts it, so she's got a special soft spot for me.

The moment we turned up at Tash's place, Peta appeared and we all knew straight away that we would be in for a laugh.

"Hello, you lot," said Peta, her eyes lighting up. "Shall I show you my new baby?"

"Oh, have you got a new doll?" asked Jaimini, trying to take an interest.

"Snot a doll. Sa baby," Peta corrected her, looking very teacherish with her hands on her hips, and wearing a heavy frown.

"Oh, sorry," said Jaimini, as Luce hid behind her so Peta wouldn't see her amusement.

"I fink somebody is being rather silly," Peta then informed us, doing an even better impression of a teacher. She marched up to Luce, who was still shaking with laughter behind Jaimini, and slapped her hard on the leg.

"Ouch! That hurt," Luce complained.

"Don't go over the top now, Peta," warned Tash. "Go and get your doll ... baby, I mean, and show it to us quickly, then we're going to make a cake. OK?"

"It's asleep. It's not ready to wake up yet, so you'll have to come upstairs to look. OK?"

We nodded and trooped obediently after her. Peta was acting like a guide in a stately home. She waited until we'd all crowded into her tiny bedroom, then she shut the door and put a finger on her lips.

"Ssh! Talk very quietly because she wakes up when you talk normal."

Again we nodded, trying not to smile as we looked all round for the baby. I must have looked above my head without thinking, because Peta informed me with great scorn in her voice that babies didn't sleep on ceilings. We were all having more and more difficulty not laughing by this time. The trouble was, we know Peta, and if she thinks people are laughing at her, she does one of two things. Either she goes off into a big tantrum, making life hell for everyone, or she gets completely overexcited and becomes more and more hyper to try and get even more laughs out of her audience. Then she ends up by breaking things or hurting herself. She wears out poor Helen, her mother.

"Are you behaving yourself up there, Peta?" Helen's voice broke into our respectful silence for the doll.

Peta didn't answer, but just rolled her eyes as though her mum should have known better than to call out like that when a baby was asleep. Just when we'd come to the conclusion that the doll was a figment of Peta's imagination, she suddenly dramatically flung open her cupboard door to reveal a sort of home-made hammock.

The hammock was made from a silk scarf that had been twisted round a knob at one side of the cupboard. The other end of the scarf had been poked over a rusty-looking nail in a piece of wood at the other side. The doll lay in the hammock, but we could only actually see its legs, which were sticking up at right-angles.

Peta grinned at us, then her little face snapped back into its serious look as she put her finger to her lips again. We all crept forwards to have a better look.

"What's her name?" I whispered.

"Conker," Peta told me gravely. I didn't dare catch Andy's eye, but one of the others couldn't help giggling behind me. "She does proper wee-wees and crying," Peta added.

Knowing we couldn't stand much more, Tash said, "Right, we're going to make a cake now, Peta. You stay here and look after Conker."

Then we all trooped back downstairs and waited till the kitchen door was closed behind us before we collapsed into fits of laughter. Surprisingly, Peta only reappeared once when we were making the cake, and that was to lick out the bowl. We then phoned Fen at the café to tell her that we were going to Miss Farrant's and to check she didn't mind, which she didn't.

Miss Farrant was very slow to come to the door and I got quite a shock when I saw her because she looked so grey. I don't mean her hair, because that had been grey for ages, I mean her skin. And her eyes looked watery. She was moving very slowly and the others all went quiet. The problem was that they didn't know Miss Farrant as well as I did, so they weren't really sure what to say to her when it was obvious she was so ill. Seeing her like this made me regret bringing them along, too. We sat down and showed her our cake. We'd actually iced some words on to it. It said, MISS FARRANT WITH LOVE.

She smiled round at us all and thanked us very much, then told me to go and make some tea and cut up the cake. This was a bad sign. When I'd visited her before, she'd always made the tea herself and I'd sat in her kitchen chatting to her while she got out the cups and everything. Tash quickly offered to make the tea instead, and Luce and Jaimini went with her to help. Andy stayed with me. I had a big lump in my throat because I couldn't bear to see Miss Farrant in this state, and it was as though Andy knew I was sad and wanted to stay with me to check I was all right.

I told Miss Farrant all about school and about David Laws having been given my place as leader of the orchestra by Mr Grote. Miss Farrant didn't know Mr Grote but said that she thought he'd soon change his mind and give me back my position when he realized his mistake. Miss Farrant smiled at me when she said that, but it was a smile that only just reached her eyes, as though the effort of smiling was enormous.

The others were quick to make the tea, and Luce handed round the plates while Jaimini sliced the cake. Miss Farrant didn't want any. I asked her how her guinea pig was and she said he was fine, though she hadn't handled him for quite a while. A neighbour had been seeing to him for the last week or so. We all went out into the garden to look at the guinea pig in his run and to give him some more hay, and I was the first one to go back into the house. Miss Farrant had fallen asleep so I put a finger to my lips to tell the others to come in quietly.

"We'd better go," mouthed Tash, and I nodded. So we cleared away the tea things as quietly as we could, then the others crept out. I hung back because I felt too sad to leave Miss Farrant like this. She was more ill than I'd ever seen her and I could feel tears pricking the backs of my eyes. What if I never saw her again? On an impulse I went back over to her, bent down and gave her a kiss on her grey cheek.

Her eyes flickered open, but it took her a moment to focus properly on me. When she did, the tears gathered in her eyes once more.

"Come and see me on your own, dear," she whispered. "And … make it … quite soon, hmm?"

She tried to smile, but I couldn't smile back. My throat was too tight and painful to speak, so I just nodded. I gave her another kiss and a tear rolled out of my eye, down to my lips and on to Miss Farrant's face.

"My niece is coming tomorrow, but come on

Monday, dear. You never know, I'll probably be up making the tea again by then."

She was only trying to cheer me up. She would never be making tea again. She was dying, and in that brief moment when our eyes met, I saw that she knew *I* knew, too.

"I'll come straight after school," I managed to say in shuddery breaths. "I'll be here by four o'clock." Miss Farrant held my hand very tightly, then let it go suddenly as though she'd used up every last gram of energy she had. This little gesture only made me sadder and I wanted Monday to come very quickly.

"See you on Monday, dear."

I nodded, because by then there was no way I could speak. My face was struggling not to fold into crying, and as soon as I was out of sight of Miss Farrant I started wiping the tears off my face with the back of my hand. Andy was waiting for me by the gate and the others had thoughtfully gone on.

"I should have come on my own," I said to Andy through my tears, which were blinding me and rolling down my face by then. Andy tucked her arm through mine.

"Do you want to go back and spend a bit of time with her?"

"I don't think she wants me to. I think she's too tired to stay awake. I'm going to see her on Monday."

"Maybe she's just going through a bad patch at the moment."

"She said she'd probably be up and about making the tea on Monday, but she won't. She's dying, Andy. I can tell. And I can't bear it." I stopped and covered my eyes because I was really crying by then.

Andy didn't say anything until I'd taken my hands away and started walking again.

"I'll help you bear it," she said. We didn't speak any more all the way back to Tash's. It's a funny thing with Andy, but you know how brave and daring she is? Well, it was almost as though she was staying silent because she was concentrating on trying to transmit some of her courage to me. All I know is that by the time we'd got back to Tash's I was almost back to normal. Almost, not completely.

Fen joined us shortly afterwards and Tash immediately told Fen that she wanted to show her something in her room, but I knew what she was up to. She wanted to warn Fen that I was upset and that Miss Farrant was really ill. Sure enough, when they came down Fen didn't say a word about our visit to Miss Farrant's. That proved that I was right because it wasn't normal not to mention our visit when we'd only just got back. The others had obviously been talking together, too, because everyone was making a big effort to keep me cheerful.

We played *The Game of Life*, and loads of card games, then we watched a video and ate pizza. Andy was the only one who was acting completely normally. I thought about this much later as I lay in a sleeping-bag on Tash's sitting-room floor, surrounded by all the others. The others couldn't quite cope with my sadness and tried to blot it out with jokes and having fun together. But Andy wasn't scared of the thought of Miss Farrant dying, or of my grief.

We'd been chatting for ages, but the chattering had stopped and I think I was the only one awake. We'd left a little lamp on in the corner and from its faint light I could see that Jaimini and Fen were definitely asleep. Luce was too far away for me to see, and Andy and Tash were facing the other way, but Tash's shoulder was going up and down very slowly so I reckoned she was definitely asleep. I watched Luce for several seconds and when her right arm suddenly plonked on the floor, I knew she was asleep, too. Then I watched Andy, but she didn't seem to be moving at all.

"Are you awake, Lee?" she suddenly whispered into the gloom.

"Yeah."

I waited for a moment to see if she'd say anything else, but she didn't, and I wanted her to know that I wasn't lying there crying or anything.

"I *am* OK, Andy. Honestly. Go to sleep."

"I'm just waiting till *you're* asleep," she replied in a very matter-of-fact tone. That's the amazing thing about Andy. Everything she does that's strong or brave, she does quietly. For all I knew she might have been really tired, but because she'd thought that I might need a friendly shoulder to cry on, she'd deliberately stayed awake.

"Thanks," I whispered, then I must have fallen asleep because the next thing I knew, it was morning.

Chapter 5

"I wish the café opened on Sundays," Luce remarked cheerfully and loudly, waking us all up on Sunday morning.

"Go back to sleep," Jaimini told her, with a yawn, before she disappeared inside her sleeping-bag.

"It's misty," Andy commented quietly.

"How can you tell when the curtains are drawn?" asked Tash, and I was wondering that, too.

"It feels it," replied Andy.

Fen didn't say a thing. She'd opened her eyes briefly when Luce had first spoken, then she'd shut them again.

Luce leapt up and rushed to the window, pulling the curtains open with a flourish. "She's right. The girl's got extrasensory perception, that's all I can say."

"Good," came a grunt from Fen's direction.

"Good what?" Luce asked.

"Good, that that's all you can say," came the mumbled response.

"Why?" Luce persisted.

"Because some of us are trying to get some sleep around here!" Jaimini came out in sympathy with Fen.

"And some of us are very grumpy in the mornings," retorted Luce.

"Don't be so hard on yourself, Luce," Andy said, and I could hear the smile in her voice.

"Not me! Those two!" squeaked Luce, indignantly, rising to the bait as Andy knew she would.

"I'm hungry," I said.

"You don't look it," was Luce's weird reply.

"How can you *look* hungry?" asked Tash.

"You just can. And anyway, how come you only ask questions in the morning?"

"I don't only ask questions," Tash said, quite forcefully for Tash.

"Yes, you do. You asked how come Andy knew it was misty with the curtains drawn, and now you're asking how you can look hungry."

"That's only two questions. Anyway, how *did* you know?" Tash asked, turning to Andy.

"My God," said Luce, pressing her nose against the window-pane. "I can't see a thing."

"That's because you've breathed all over the

glass, I expect," Jaimini mumbled from inside her sleeping-bag.

"I have not breathed all over it. It's misty," said Luce.

"What a ridiculous conversation," Fen said in a muffled sort of groan, and at that point those of us who were awake got up, while Fen and Jaimini had another hour's sleep.

Later, while we were having breakfast, Luce repeated her original opening line.

"I wish the café was open on Sundays. We could go down there and meet up with Rob, Chris and Guy."

I felt myself go pink. It was all right for the others. They could meet up with Rob, Chris and Guy, but I wouldn't be welcome, because Rob really thought I'd dobbed on him. If I had the guts I'd ask Mr Grote to tell Rob it wasn't me. I wouldn't dare do that, of course, because that would mean that Mr Grote would have to admit that he'd just taken a lucky guess and been right. I wondered whether I might have the courage to approach Mr Grote at break-time and tell him what had happened, and I kept thinking about this plan all through Sunday, so that by the end of the day, I'd got used to the idea and decided that I'd go ahead with it.

Monday morning assembly was supposed to be my big chance to change Mr Grote's opinion of me. I stood nervously but determinedly on the stage with the two girls who were playing their recorders with me. I had done an hour's practice on Sunday evening, and for once I felt confident that nothing could go wrong. The only thing that was wrong at that moment was that there was absolutely no sign of Mr Grote, and everybody else was present and waiting.

"Where's Mr Grote?" I whispered to one of the girls who was playing recorder.

"Dunno. Think Ms Chambers wants us to get on with it, though."

I looked over to Ms Chambers and she was nodding at me and smiling. It would have seemed very babyish to ask her where Mr Grote was, so there was nothing for it but to start playing and hope that he turned up during the piece. This time, nothing would faze me. I kept glancing towards the door as I played but it never opened, and then when the piece came to an end I was filled with a horrible, depressing feeling. My big chance to improve things had come and gone. Everybody clapped like mad and Ms Chambers praised us, but her praise slid off me like jelly off a spoon.

Second lesson on Monday was music and I couldn't help feeling optimistic as I went into the music room because I'd suddenly remembered that Mrs Merle might be back. It would be fantastic if she was, then everything would go back to normal. The sight of Mr Grote bending over his books and papers seemed worse than ever, I'd been so hoping to see Mrs Merle.

He didn't look up properly until we were all in our places, then he clasped his hands together and let his eyes slowly go round the whole class. His head was thrust forwards slightly as though this was helping him take in every single thing about us all. It was most unnerving. I didn't dare turn to look at any of the others, but I could just about see Tash out of the corner of my eye and she looked as alarmed as I was.

"Right! Twelve-part piece! Instruments!" Mr Grote suddenly announced to the silence. Then he turned to the cupboard where various glocks and xylophones, chime bars and tambourines and things were kept. I hesitantly got up and approached the cupboard, along with Guy and another boy called William, and a girl called Alex. Mrs Merle always had monitors to help give out the instruments and it was our turn this term.

"Thank you, but I think we'll have a bit of a change," said Mr Grote, turning round and seeing us behind him. "Leah, go and sit down. David, would you like to come and take her place?"

Mr Grote smiled for the first time. I couldn't believe it. I waited to see if he was going swap any of the other monitors, but no, it was only me. I looked at Andy and saw her eyes narrow as she folded her arms and slumped further down into her seat. This was Andy at her most disapproving and suspicious. Fen and Tash shrugged their shoulders and gave me sympathetic smiles.

Alex plonked the biggest glock down in front of me, because whenever we were about to play a difficult piece with lots of parts in it for all the different instruments, I usually got to play this big glock as I was the most advanced on a keyboard instrument. David sometimes played a glock or a xylophone too, only this time he'd got left with a pair of Indian bells.

When all the instruments had been given out, Mr Grote gave us another of his neck-thrust-forwards inspections of the class. "Thank you, but I think we'll have a change," he said for the second time in under five minutes, and I felt my blood run cold. I knew what was about to happen even before it did. "The two girls at the back swap instruments with the two boys next to you, and Leah and David swap instruments."

I stood up with quaking knees, but David managed to get to me before I was even out of my place. He had his back to Mr Grote as he put his Indian bells on my table and rather awkwardly picked up the glock. "Sorry," he mouthed, and he really did look sorry, which surprised me, because I thought he was quite enjoying being teacher's pet. Perhaps I'd been wrong to think that. Now that he was so close to me I had the chance to see his hand. Although he was managing to hold the glock, it was his left hand doing the bulk of the work. His right hand was draped round the glock but not all his fingers were actually clasping it. I wondered if he'd hurt his hand or something.

It was probably the most boring music lesson I'd ever sat through, because I could play my part easily and Mr Grote never asked me to help anyone else. David managed the glock fine, but he was playing with his left hand. I wondered whether he was actually left-handed or if he was having to use his left hand because his right hand couldn't manage. It was strange that I'd never noticed anything wrong with David's hand before Friday night's concert. Although, when I thought about it, perhaps it wasn't all that odd because I'd never really taken any notice of David before Mr Grote came. I knew he played the violin but he wasn't particularly advanced, yet now all of a sudden Mr Grote seemed to be grooming David for stardom. I couldn't work it out.

At the end of the lesson Andy stopped me in the corridor. "You're not going to put up with this, are you, Leah?"

"You mean, Mr Grote picking on me?"

"Exactly."

"Well, what can I do?"

"You can go and ask him if there's any particular reason why he's got it in for you."

"Oh, Andy, I wouldn't dare. You know me." I was half hoping that Andy might offer to say something on my behalf, but she thought it was up to me.

"There's no way I can help you out with this, Lee. Mr Grote would just tell me to mind my own business if I started defending you or complaining about the way he's treating you."

"Yes, I know, but like I said, I daren't confront him myself. I don't want to make matters worse. I was thinking of waiting to see whether he put me back as leader of the orchestra tomorrow."

"Tomorrow? I thought orchestra was on Fridays."

"It is normally, but Mr Grote's changed it this week, for some reason."

"Leah, can I talk to you for a minute, please?" I turned to see David Laws standing there.

"I'll see you down on the netball courts," said Andy tactfully, as she hurried lightly down the corridor.

"Look, Leah, I'm really sorry about the way Mr Grote is carrying on. It doesn't seem at all fair to me, and I just ... wanted you to know that..."

He was looking at me so sincerely, I felt instantly sorry for him. After all, it wasn't David's fault that Mr Grote had decided to take me down a few pegs and put David up a few, was it?

"That's OK, I'm surviving," I said, with a friendly smile.

"I've been really worried that people will start to think it's my fault."

"Oh, don't worry about that," I reassured him. "I'll make sure that people realize I'm not taking it personally."

"Are you going to speak to him at all? I mean, are you going to say anything about me being the leader of the orchestra or anything?"

"I considered it, but I don't think I'll bother. After all, Mrs Merle will be back soon, I expect, then I presume things will go back to normal."

I couldn't help noticing David's eyes at that point. He seemed to want to look anywhere but at my face.

"What's the matter, David? Do you know something that I don't?"

"I heard Mr Grote talking with Ms Chambers and it doesn't look as though Mrs Merle is coming back for a week or so, maybe more."

"Why? What's the matter with Mrs Merle?"

"I'm not sure ... exactly."

David was holding his file in his left hand and his right hand was in his pocket. Did I dare to ask him what had happened to it? The only trouble was, what if he'd been born with it like that? He might think I was being really personal. It might be something that he was very sensitive about. With his next words, I realized that I must have been more obvious than I'd thought.

"Were you wondering about this?" he said, pulling his hand out of his pocket and holding it in front of me, where it dangled down from his wrist.

"Well, I..."

"I broke it, you see."

"Oh, so it *will* get better?"

"Doesn't look like it."

"Why?"

"I broke it about four years ago but it was such a bad break that it never went back to normal. The nerves were damaged and I got an infection in it, so now I haven't got any sensation in a lot of my hand and fingers."

"But you can play the violin?"

"Yes, thank goodness it wasn't my left hand. I'm left-handed, so at least I can still write and everything. Holding a bow isn't all that easy, but it *is* possible. I'd hate to give up playing the violin because I love it. I used to play the piano, too, but I've had to give that up."

"I'm really sorry, David. I had no idea."

"It's OK. I manage. Listen, I'm playing the violin at a festival next week. Mr Grote told me about it earlier. I wondered if you wanted to play the piano part. It's a proper duet for violin and piano, not just a piano accompaniment."

"Yes, of course I will," I said, feeling glad that there was something I could do which would be helpful. It must have been so awful for David to have to put up with his hand being almost useless, when he was so keen on music.

"The music's quite easy, so you won't need to practise it till the last minute."

"OK, that's fine," I said. "And I'm really sorry about your hand."

"They were supposed to be operating on it, but at my last hospital appointment they said I've got to wait till I'm fifteen. That's two more years. I wish no one had ever said anything about operations, then I wouldn't have got my hopes up that they were going to operate now."

There didn't seem to be anything more that I could say, but while he'd been talking I'd come to a decision. If Mr Grote wanted to swap me back as leader of the orchestra, I was going to refuse. That was the least I could do for poor David – let him be leader of the orchestra. I ran down to the netball courts, counting my blessings all the way.

"Where've you been?" asked Luce, the moment I sat down.

"You're so nosy, Luce," Jaimini informed her friend.

"It's not nosiness, it's curiosity," Luce retorted.

"Talking to David Laws," I answered, realizing that Andy, in her usual discreet way, hadn't said where I was.

"David Laws? Mr Grote's pet?"

"We've been telling her about the music lesson," Fen filled me in. "Mr Grote really does seem to have it in for you, Leah. Why do you think it could be?"

"I haven't the faintest idea," I answered, "but I don't really mind, if it gives David a chance to show himself a bit."

"Methinks I detect a faint whiff of sorry-for-Davidness," said Luce, narrowing her eyes and looking thoroughly ridiculous.

"You're right, Detective Edmunson," I joked. "I do feel sorry for David." Then I told them everything that David had told me about his hand.

"Poor thing," said Tash, looking really sad.

"I agree it must be awful, but it's not really a big enough reason for you to be dropped as leader of the orchestra, is it?" Fen said.

"And what's all this I've been hearing about even dropping you as one of the monitors?" said Jaimini. "I could understand Mr Grote feeling sorry for David, but at the same time he seems to be victimizing you and that's ridiculous."

"I agree with Jaimes," said Luce.

I didn't need to ask Andy what she thought

because she'd made it quite clear when we'd come out of the music lesson.

"I presume Mrs Merle must have given Mr Grote some notes about all the pupils and the work we've covered and everything. They usually do that for supply teachers, don't they?" Fen went on. "Mr Grote's obviously read about David and feels really sorry for him. Maybe it's just coincidence that he's giving David everything that you used to do, Leah."

"I doubt it," said Andy, staring straight ahead.

"So what do *you* think, then?" I finally asked her.

"Not sure," she answered, because as I've already explained, Andy doesn't like giving opinions until she's sure of them. I could tell from her expression that she was intrigued by all this, though. Personally, I didn't really care any more about Mr Grote. I was just happy that David would be in the limelight, at least until Mrs Merle came back.

I saw David at lunchtime. He was on his own as usual, so I went and sat with him. The others came too, but I could tell they didn't really want to. I felt proud of myself that for once I was being a leader and doing what I felt was right.

"Why don't you come down to the café after school?" I suggested brightly to David. "You know we all work there?"

"No, I didn't realize," he said. So we told him all about how our Café Club had got started. Well, to be honest *I* was the one doing most of the talking. The others seemed embarrassed to be seen talking to David. In fact, Luce went over to join Robert Taylor when he appeared with Guy and Chris at the next table. I didn't care. It was such a nice change for me to be sticking to my principles and doing what I felt was right even though other people might not necessarily agree with me.

After school I walked down to the café with David, and the others walked on ahead of us. Andy stayed with me and David for a bit, but then she said she was going to jog, so I explained to David that Andy often did this. I didn't want him to feel hurt and think that Andy was bored with his company.

Luce was on duty, and the café was really full. I love the atmosphere in the café when it's like that. The only thing I didn't particularly like about this day was that Rob Taylor and his two mates were sitting at the table next to us. They did their usual thing of saying "hi" to all the others but not to me. They also made a point of ignoring David as well, I noticed, until he suddenly said something to Rob.

"Hey, you know your torch-pen?"

"Uh-huh."

"I bought one at the weekend."

"Yeah?" Rob couldn't help showing interest now. It was funny watching him wrestling with himself to keep up his hostile front, but not quite so hostile that David didn't feel like giving him the information he wanted. "Where d'you get it? I looked everywhere for one because Gloaty Grote say's he's mislaid mine. He assures me he's going to have a good look for it, but he says that it's my own fault for having it in class in the first place. I said that it was the pen I write with, so what was wrong with that? And he said that pens like that with gadgets on them were against the rules. I asked my tutor and she said Gloaty Grote was right. School rules make me puke."

"We went away for the weekend and I found mine in one of those gift shops that sell all sorts of stuff like it."

"Oh ... right." Rob had turned away. He wasn't interested in David Laws any more, especially since David was sitting with me. He was so selfish, Rob. I'd like to see how he would have coped with David's problems.

"You can have my pen, if you want," David said suddenly, and that really got our attention. All of us girls, as well as Rob, Chris and Guy gawped at David as though he'd announced that his family had won the Lottery.

"Do you mean that?" Rob asked, going back to

his "half-and-half" face, which was such a picture.

"Yeah, sure," said David. He even smiled at Rob, and the sight of Rob's face then was almost too much to look at! He was gobsmacked.

"Oh right, thanks very much then," he stuttered, looking distinctly embarrassed. I felt really proud of David. It was such a nice gesture of his. I looked round at the others and saw that they didn't know what to make of it. David was digging into his school bag, with the attention of all of us on him. Out came the torch-pen. He handed it straight to Rob.

"What's this?" asked Rob, scrutinizing the pen.

"Oh, it's a sticker. They sold those in the same shop, so I bought one to stick on the pen."

Rob's eyes didn't leave the pen, but a shadow crossed his face. I automatically glanced at Andy to see if she'd noticed anything, but she was leaning back in her chair saying something to Luce, who was walking by with a tray of drinks. When Rob looked up, his eyes met mine. I couldn't tell what he was thinking; all I knew was that it was something important.

"Lee!" Andy suddenly said, grabbing my arm. I wondered what on earth could be the matter. "You're supposed to be at Miss Farrant's!"

"Omigod!"

I didn't waste time explaining my sudden exit to David, because I knew Andy and the others would take care of that. I just took to my heels and belted off. My watch said quarter to five. That meant that it would be five past by the time I got to Miss Farrant's. She'd think I wasn't coming. I'd been very specific about being there at four o'clock. How could I have forgotten poor Miss Farrant? I felt so guilty and anxious. I couldn't bear the thought of her sitting there sadly looking at the clock.

Miss Farrant always left the back door unlocked and I always knocked and went straight in, so it was quite a shock to find the back door locked. I knocked loudly on the door and when there was no answer I really hammered on it, in case she'd fallen asleep. When there was still no answer I walked up the steps to the bay window at the back and peered into the sitting-room. The room was all neat and tidy. Miss Farrant was not in her usual chair.

She *had* to be somewhere in the house. She'd told me to come on Monday, so she wouldn't have gone out, surely. I tried rapping on the back door one last time, then walked round to the front, feeling miserable. I was on the point of trudging off home, when my eye caught something on the front door. It was a note. I rushed over to read it.

Leah,

Sorry, dear. I've had to go into St Prestlins

hospital. It might be best if you phone the hospital, rather than just turning up. I know how busy you are, so just come when you can. You know I always love to see you.

Your friend,

Margaret Farrant

Miss Farrant had had to go into hospital! Why? This was a million times worse than my nightmare. I closed my eyes and said a prayer. *Please don't let her die, please don't let her die.* Then I rushed home as fast as I could, saying another prayer that Dad would be home with the car. I had to get to the hospital straight away.

"Dad! Thank goodness you're home. Can you do me a big favour? Please, Dad?"

"Calm down, Leah," said Mum, following me from the kitchen to the living-room with a tea towel and bowl in her hands.

"What's going on?" Dad asked. Poor old Dad was baffled about what was going on at the best of times, but now he really did look confused.

"I've just been to see Miss Farrant, but she wasn't there and she left me a note to say that she's been taken into hospital. I've got to see her. I'm afraid that..."

"Calm down, Leah," Mum repeated, but her arm went round my shoulder.

"Catch, Dad," called out my sister, Kim, who

had jumped up from the settee, recognizing the urgency and panic in my voice. Kim knows me well and she was helping me to get some action going. Dad caught the car keys she'd thrown at him and this was just what he needed to get motivated.

"Let's be on our way, then," he said, in his usual, lovely way. I flashed Kim a grateful look and she gave me a fingers-crossed sign back. I knew what she meant. She meant, *I hope Miss Farrant is OK when you get there, Leah.*

Dad talked about this and that all the way to the hospital. It's very relaxing, being with Dad. He never gets intense about anything. I didn't mind talking like this. It was better than silence. The moment we got to the hospital, though, I leapt out of the car and rushed for the main entrance.

"You go on. I'll find you," Dad called, and I didn't need telling twice. I rushed up to the woman at reception and asked where Margaret Farrant would be. She asked if I was a relative and I was about to say no, then I changed my mind and told a lie. Something told me that I wouldn't be allowed to see her unless I said I was a relative, so I said I was her niece and hoped that the woman thought I looked the part. My heart was beating like mad because of telling the lie, and also because of the whole horror of this situation. I just wanted to see that she was all right, then I'd relax.

The receptionist turned her back on me, picked up a phone and spoke softly into it. I thought this was a bad sign and I held my breath all the time until she'd finished talking.

"Someone will be along in a moment to show you the way, dear."

Her smile was too kind. Oh, no. *Please don't let me be too late.* My face felt cold as though my cheeks hadn't got any blood in them. A nurse was approaching me. I studied her eyes. She didn't see me looking at first, and her face was one big concentrated frown, then she noticed me, and she gave me one of those sympathetic, deeply-sorry smiles. It was for my benefit. I knew it. She was sorry for me. She had to give some terrible news. I couldn't look at her any more. In fact, I couldn't focus on anything. Her white uniform was dazzling me and making me dizzy. My knees were buckling and then the hard floor was rising up to hit me. It hurt, but not as much as the pain inside my chest.

Chapter 6

"Feeling better now, dear?"

The truth was, I didn't know if I was feeling better or not because for a few seconds I couldn't think where I was or what had happened.

"You fainted."

I looked up then and saw the kind face of the nurse.

"I've came to see Miss Farrant. Is she...?"

"She's very poorly, but you can see her."

I stood up and the nurse kept a guiding hand on my arm for the first few steps. All I could think was, *Thank goodness I'm not too late*.

"In here," said the nurse a few minutes later, when we'd walked along two corridors, up some stairs, down another corridor and come to a small room with just one bed.

Miss Farrant was lying on her side, facing the door, but her eyes were closed. Her face seemed greyer than ever. Tears pricked the backs of my eyes. The nurse bent down and said softly, "Your niece is here to see you, Miss Farrant." Miss Farrant didn't open her eyes and my heart started hammering in fear again. The nurse bent even closer to Miss Farrant's face, then straightened up and asked me what my name was.

"Leah," I replied in a small voice, and that's when Miss Farrant opened her eyes and moved her hand just a fraction. I went forward and took her hand. "It's Leah," I repeated, so she wouldn't be in any doubt.

"I'll leave you for a few minutes," said the nurse. "Just a few minutes, mind, dear, because your aunt needs to rest."

Miss Farrant didn't move, except to give my hand a squeeze.

"Sorry, I had to say I was your niece," I said the moment the nurse had gone.

"There's a chair by the door, I think," she answered in a weak voice. I rushed over to get it, not wanting to lose any time arguing that I was fine standing when I'd only been given a few precious minutes.

"Sorry you had a wasted journey, Leah."

"No, it wasn't … it wasn't wasted. I know you said I should phone first, but I wanted to come straight away."

"That was clever of you, thinking to say you were my niece."

For the first time her old face creased into a smile and this time it did reach her eyes. I felt a glimmer of hope. Maybe she would be all right, after all. Maybe this was just a temporary relapse. I desperately wanted to know why she had to be in hospital but it was difficult to know how to ask.

"I was quite frightened when I saw the note on the door..."

"Sorry, dear. I didn't mean to alarm you."

"Did you call an ambulance?"

"My neighbour did. She hadn't seen me for a couple of days and she was frightened by the sound of my breathing. She said she thought I looked awful, which I probably did!" Again Miss Farrant smiled, and I managed to smile back. "She also said she was going to call my niece, so when the nurse said it was my niece here to see me, I believed her."

"Were you all right when your niece came yesterday?"

"She didn't come. Typical!"

I had been holding Miss Farrant's hand all the time, but when she told me about her niece I felt so choked I couldn't help squeezing a bit tighter.

"Don't worry about that," said Miss Farrant, wrinkling her nose. "She's not my very favourite person in the world, I can assure you. You're my favourite, so I'm considering myself very lucky at the moment!"

The lump in my throat was coming back. I still hadn't found out what I wanted to know. I could see the nurse returning, and Dad's face was bobbing in and out of view at the window in the door. I knew Dad. He would be weighing up whether or not to come in.

"I think we'd better let your young visitor go," said the nurse. I noticed that she didn't say "let your niece go". Maybe she'd been talking to Dad, and he'd told her I was just a friend.

"I'll come back again tomorrow," I said to Miss Farrant with the best smile I could manage. All I really wanted to do was burst into sobs and hug her and tell her not to die.

"Thank you so much for coming, dear. I can't tell you how much better I feel now I've seen you. Take care, won't you?"

"I'll be back to see you tomorrow," I said insistently, because I just wanted her to reply with a nice, bright "See you tomorrow", to show me that she thought she would still be here.

"Yes, dear, if you've got time. That would be lovely."

"Of course I've got time." I kissed her grey cheek and didn't look at her eyes because I didn't trust myself not to cry. I couldn't even say bye, because my voice would have shaken the tears out of my eyes, so I hurried out to Dad. He took one look at my face, thanked the nurse, and followed me back out to the car without saying anything. I was walking really quickly because I couldn't bear being in that hospital a second longer.

"Not so good then?" Dad ventured when we'd set off.

I shook my head.

"Brave girl," he said, and because no other words passed between us for the rest of the journey, I had plenty of time to wonder whether he meant that I was a brave girl for managing not to cry or whether he was telling me to *be* brave. He put the radio on after he'd spoken. There was a programme on about frogs and toads, which didn't have any awful associations and was just about interesting enough to penetrate my gloom.

That night I had the nightmare again and woke up in a cold sweat. The relief of waking up was very quickly knocked out of me by the memory of Miss Farrant lying so ill in hospital, and at breakfast I asked Mum if I could phone the hospital and find out how she was. Mum told me to get ready for school and said she would phone herself. I knew exactly why she wanted to do that. She was afraid Miss Farrant had died in the night and she didn't want me to find out from a nurse on the phone.

I pretended to go into my room but then I crept back and sat on the top stair so I could hear Mum on the phone downstairs. I couldn't keep the bottoms of my legs still, they were trembling so much.

"Hello, I'm enquiring about Miss Margaret Farrant, a cancer patient. Could you tell me how she is this morning, please? … My daughter, Leah, came to see her yesterday … Yes … Is she? … Yes … I see … Yes … Thank you very much. Goodbye."

I rushed downstairs and placed myself right in front of Mum.

"She's the same as yesterday, love."

"No better?"

"But no worse."

At least my worst fears were over for the moment.

At school, before registration, I told Andy about Miss Farrant and my visit to the hospital.

"If she's in a lot of pain, it'll be a relief when she dies, Leah," Andy told me softly. I knew that, but it didn't help me to feel any better. I noticed Andy had said "when she dies", not "*if* she dies".

"What have you done to your hair?" Luce asked me, coming into the room at that moment.

"Nothing… Oh, no! Does it look awful? I forgot to brush it this morning. My mind was on other things."

"It's not its usual silky, swinging self, that's for sure," said Luce, with a grin. I began to feel around in my school bag for my brush.

"No, don't brush it. Keep it like that. It makes me feel much better about my own hair," Luce went on.

"That's funny. It doesn't seem to be here," I said, rummaging around at the bottom of the bag, and because I couldn't believe it, I tipped the entire contents of my bag out on to the desk. The brush was nowhere to be seen. It couldn't possibly be missing. I'd kept that same hairbrush in my bag since year six!

"Here, borrow my comb, if you want," said Luce, tossing me her wide-toothed comb, which I could see at a glance wouldn't be much good on my fine hair. I thanked her anyway.

At morning break, I was about to go out with the others down to our usual place, when Robert Taylor came up to me. I felt myself tensing at the very sight of him, so you can imagine my shock when he said, "That thing you played on the violin yesterday in assembly sounded really good."

"Oh ... thanks."

"How long have you been playing?"

"Er ... quite a few years."

"I didn't know anyone could make a violin sound like that. Look, Leah ... I..."

"Oh, there you are, Leah!" It was David. "I was wondering if you could have a look at my violin. It's got a rattle of some sort, and I can't work out what it is."

"Yeah, course."

I examined the violin and managed to shake a tiny speck of dirt or something out of it, then when I looked up again I realized Rob had gone.

"Where's Rob, David?"

"He just went. I don't think he likes me."

"Of course he does. In fact, I should think he *really* likes you after you gave him your torch-pen."

"I just wish I didn't have this stupid, useless hand. I'm sure people think that *I'm* stupid and useless when they see that my hand doesn't work properly."

"No, they don't, David. I didn't even notice your hand until..." I trailed off because I didn't want to embarrass him by mentioning the concert at Limendowling.

"Until I dropped Mr Grote's music, right?"

"No, it wasn't that. It was just that you were on the stage, and, you know..."

I felt terrible, and more determined than ever to make sure that David kept his place as leader of the orchestra. What did it matter whether I was leader or not?

Andy came rushing up to me. "Ms Chambers wants to see you in her office now."

"Me? Why?" I started worrying about what I might have done wrong. Ms Chambers is the head-teacher, and it's most unusual to be called to her office. It's nearly always when you've done something really good or really bad.

"Come in," she said when I knocked on the door. Imagine my shock when I went in to find Mrs Merle standing there. She said hello to me, but I knew immediately that there was something wrong. Her smile was so forced, it made me shiver.

"I'll come straight to the point. Mrs Merle was burgled on Friday, Leah," said Ms Chambers in a very serious voice.

"Burgled!" I was horrified.

"Not much was taken, but those items which were stolen are very valuable and very precious to Mrs Merle."

I gulped, remembering how I'd tiptoed round Mrs Merle's house on Friday afternoon. It hadn't been burgled when *I'd* been there. It was all neat and tidy. I was on the point of saying this, but Mrs Merle was speaking.

"My music box was taken, Leah," she said in a tight voice. "Also my metronome, and a couple of CDs."

Again I gulped. My brain was going mad trying to follow the conversation and work out what was coming. They both looked so strict and grave. Why were they telling me all this? They didn't suspect me, did they? The moment the thought had popped into my head, I couldn't get rid of it. Someone must have seen me go in to

Mrs Merle's house. It was a horrible, sickening coincidence that the very two items I had admired the last time I'd been there were the ones that were missing. In fact, I had more than admired them. I had gone right over the top, saying how lucky Mrs Merle was to own such beautiful things, and how the music box would be my pride and joy if I owned it. Mrs Merle was giving me a very odd look. That proved it.

"Is this your hairbrush, Leah?" Ms Chambers said suddenly, holding up my brush. She'd had it hidden behind her desk. My eyes must have shown that I recognized it, but fast as anything I changed my expression. Something told me if I wasn't careful I was about to fall right into a clever trap.

"It looks like mine, but now I look at it properly, I don't think it is, actually."

"I think it is, Leah," said Ms Chambers. Her voice sounded so cold.

"No, mine's thicker than that."

"Really? You surprise me. And is your hair also thicker than this? Let's see."

She pulled a few strands of hair out of the brush, got up and came over to me. "Looks remarkably similar to me, Leah," she went on, holding the hairs next to my head. She was trying to look sympathetically and kindly at me, but it was a trap. I knew it was.

I was very scared by now, but I had to keep up the pretence, otherwise I'd be accused of burgling Mrs Merle's house. In a sudden flash I remembered the moment when I had swung round at the foot of the stairs, and my school bag had clunked hard against the banister. My hairbrush must have fallen out of my bag with the force of the bang. I felt hemmed in by their trap. A part of me was still considering telling the truth, but they'd never believe me. It would all be far too much of a coincidence: Mrs Merle's house had been burgled on Friday, the very two things I had admired had been taken, and I had been inside her house at the right time. It hadn't been me, but they would never, ever believe me.

"Leah, I want you to think carefully before answering this next question, because it's important that you tell the truth. Were you inside Mrs Merle's house on Friday?" She still wore that fake, sympathetic, I'm-your-friend look. I turned away. I mustn't trust her.

I had never thought so carefully about anything in all my life as I did about that question. If I said "yes" I would be accused of stealing; if I said "no" I would be accused of lying. Stealing seemed much worse than lying, and anyway I'd have to admit that I'd been lying about the hairbrush in the first place, if I suddenly admitted that I had been inside Mrs Merle's house on Friday.

"No," I replied, with my heart in my mouth.

"Are you quite sure?" Mrs Merle asked me. She was really pleading with her eyes for me to change my mind, but I didn't dare.

"I'm quite sure," I said, even trying to sound offended that they should accuse me in this way.

"But this hairbrush was found at the bottom of my stairs," Mrs Merle went on, acting like Ms Chambers was – encouraging me to own up. But I couldn't. They were both convinced it was me, I felt sure.

"It's not mine, I told you."

There was a long pause, while both of them stared at me, then Ms Chambers said, "Right, thank you, Leah. You can go now."

I crept out of that office feeling about three centimetres tall, and more worried than I'd felt for a very long time. This made my problem with the school orchestra seem like a problem with a dirty stain on a pair of jeans, when you'd got ten other identical pairs. I made for the loos and locked myself inside one of them.

Sitting with my knees bunched up on the lid of the toilet, and my eye sockets grinding into my kneecaps, I tried desperately to think what I should do. What would Andy do? The answer was that Andy would never be in this position in the first place. She would have left a note for Mrs Merle on the door, then Mrs Merle would have phoned her and she would have gone racing round to her house and helped her try to work out who could have committed the crime. She would have said, "Oh, *there's* my hairbrush! I was wondering where that had got to. It must have fallen out of my bag when I turned round in a hurry because I thought someone was in your kitchen."

I jumped up off the loo, unlocked the door, went out and set off down the corridor before I could change my mind. I was going straight back into that office and I would take a deep breath and say, "I know you won't believe me. I only told a lie before because I thought you'd never believe the truth, but now I'm going to tell you the truth, and I swear to God, it *is* the truth." Then I would tell them the whole story.

To get to Ms Chambers' office I had to pass the main entrance with the car park outside. A terrible sinking feeling came over me as I glanced outside and saw Mrs Merle driving away. I stood still and my head tipped forward on to my chest, as all my great resolve seeped away. There was no way I could approach Ms Chambers in her office and give her a completely changed story. She'd think I was not only a liar, but manipulative with it.

I turned and went back to the loo. I wanted so badly to go and find Andy, but something was stopping me. The problem was that Andy had helped me out when I'd nearly given Robert Taylor away; she'd comforted me about Miss Farrant and about my nightmare; about dropping a clanger with Elizabeth Driscoll *and* about not being the leader of the orchestra. She must be absolutely sick to death of me and my problems. There was no way I could confess to this latest episode in the "Stupid Behaviour of Leah Bryan" series. I would just have to sort it out for myself.

When Andy asked me where I'd been all break-time I said I'd been feeling sick and that I hadn't dared to go too far away from the loos in case I *was* sick. She seemed to believe me, probably because I looked ill with worry. I couldn't concentrate on anything for the rest of the morning, because I was trying to work out what would happen next. Would the police be brought in and my fingerprints taken? If they did that, they'd soon know I'd been lying because I must have left fingerprints all over the place in Mrs Merle's house.

I started to imagine what Mum and Dad would say. They would be devastated. But how could anyone prove it? Nobody could prove I'd taken anything, could they, because I didn't have the things at home or anywhere?

"Leah Bryan, are you on another planet?" boomed the geography teacher.

"Sorry, sir," I mumbled, going pink. I glanced round to see who had noticed my embarrassment.

Robert Taylor was watching me. I expected him to smirk, but he didn't.

"You OK?" he mouthed.

I nodded, and then wondered what he'd say if he knew what I was thinking about. If only I could confide in someone. Maybe Tash? Tash would be sympathetic and kind and understanding. No, I couldn't do that. It wouldn't be fair on Andy. I felt so alone all of a sudden...

That was it! David! I'd tell David. We'd be two lonely people together. It would make David feel much better about himself if he knew that someone else had got themselves into such a stupid and frightening situation. He might even be able to help me. Roll on, lunchtime! Then I could talk to David before orchestra started.

While all the others were going into the hall in dribs and drabs, and getting into their places for orchestra, David and I stayed outside and I told him the horrific story of Friday afternoon. He listened sympathetically, and I asked him what he would do in my place. He said that he thought maybe I ought to admit to Ms Chambers that I *had* been inside Mrs Merle's house.

"But what if they don't believe me when I promise that I didn't take the things, though?"

"I'm sure you'll be all right," was all David said to that. He had such confidence in me, it was amazing.

"Leah, can I talk to you for a minute?" It was Robert Taylor again.

"Yeah, course."

Robert looked daggers at David. "Alone," he said, rather coldly. Poor David bit his lip and looked down. I couldn't understand why Robert was being so hateful to David, and neither, obviously, could David.

"Sorry, but orchestra's starting now. Come on, David, let's go in."

David meekly followed me in, and Rob walked off for the second time that day. It was so unlike me to be so sure of myself. I couldn't believe it. Feeling sorry for David had somehow given me a kind of strength.

"Where shall we sit?" David then asked me. But I didn't need to reply because Mr Grote had arrived.

"Right, let's stick with David as leader of the orchestra. You seemed to manage very well last time, David," Mr Grote smiled.

This time I didn't mind half as much as before. I sat behind David and we started the practice. At the end of the practice Mr Grote began to explain about the festival David had mentioned. It was to take place the following week.

"It's not exactly a competition as such. It's just a grand get-together of lots of musical children from various schools in the area. They're limited for time, and so the organizers have stipulated that each school can only present two items. David has already told me that he wants to play a violin piece, and Leah has very kindly offered to play the piano part, I gather, so I need to have one other item, and I wondered about Gemma and Alex on their recorders. I could arrange that piece you played with Leah the other day for just the two of you."

Alex and Gemma nodded enthusiastically, so it was all settled. I must admit I was disappointed not to be playing on my own, because I nearly always had a solo at concerts and festivals. Still, it didn't really matter, just for once. Compared to my other problems it wasn't even worth thinking about.

David asked me if he could come to the café with me after school and I said that was fine. Then, as we were leaving the hall, Robert tried to waylay me again.

"Please, Leah, it's important. Can I speak to you on your own for a minute?"

"I don't see why you have to exclude David all the time, Robert."

"Please, Leah."

"Come on, now. The bell's gone. You should be in lesson six." That was Mr Butler, the geography teacher. For once I felt quite grateful for a teacher butting in.

"See you at the café then, Lee," said David. And I thought how nice it was that he'd used my nickname.

Robert didn't say anything, just turned and went.

Chapter 7

Walking down to the café with the others, I got myself into a terrible state again. David wasn't with me, and it was almost as though I could cope much better with life and not be so worried about everything all the time when he was by my side, but the moment he wasn't there, I was a nervous wreck. Until now, I hadn't realized what an awful mess I was in, but the full horror of the situation hit me when a word popped into my head. It was just one word that did it – *criminal*. That's what Ms Chambers and Mrs Merle thought I was – a *criminal*. I started to shake and tremble so much that Andy said she thought I ought to go home and go straight to bed.

"I'm OK, honestly. Anyway, I said I'd meet David."

"So what?" said Andy. "What's the big deal with David all of a sudden?"

I must admit Andy had shocked me because she'd sounded so aggressive. I looked to Tash and the others for a bit of moral support, and it was Tash who spoke, but not quite in the sympathetic way I had been expecting.

"I know you feel sorry for David, Lee, but don't you find it a bit weird the way he's suddenly attaching himself to you like a limpet?"

"No, I don't. I'm only glad that at long last David has managed to find himself a friend," I retorted, and Tash looked as though she was going to burst into tears. Out of the six of us, the last two you'd expect to ever exchange cross words are Tash and me.

We were practically at the café by then, thank goodness. Jaimini went in the back way because it was her turn to work, and the rest of us went in at the front. I had arranged with Dad that he would take me over to see Miss Farrant at half-past five. Mum wouldn't be back from work till then, and I didn't want to leave it till any later.

The moment we'd got a table and sat down, Robert Taylor appeared at my side.

"Leah, can I talk to you now? Please?"

I stood up to go to another table with him, as he'd said at school that he wanted to talk to me alone.

"It's OK. I don't mind the others hearing this. In fact, I'd quite like them to hear."

"So I was right. It's just David you want to exclude."

"Look, Leah, see this pen?" He pulled the pen that David had given him out of his pocket. "Well, it's *my* pen."

"I know. I saw David give it to you, remember?"

"No, I mean it's my *original* pen. David invented that whole thing about buying it and putting that sticker on it. The very moment he handed it to me I thought it looked suspiciously like my pen."

"How can you possibly tell?" I asked, feeling the faintest stirrings of unease.

"Because I peeled that sticker off that David had stuck on it. He must have put it on with super glue – it wasn't easy to get off, I can tell you. I had to use really hot water. And underneath I found two scratches. They're only little, but they make half a letter 'R'. You see, when I first got the pen, I decided to scratch my name on it, then I changed my mind because it looked a mess, and I hadn't even done the first letter."

I peered at the pen and couldn't deny that it looked like the beginning of a letter R. "So … how could David have got hold of your pen?"

"Maybe he chose his moment carefully and took it out of Gloaty Grote's bag," said Andy.

"Or maybe old Grote gave it to David as a sort of reward for dobbing on me," said Robert.

"Oh, so now you think it was David who

dobbed on you. Well, at least you've got it into your head that it wasn't Leah," said Andy, giving Robert the benefit of one of her piercing looks.

"Yeah, I'm sorry, Leah. I got that wrong. I know that now."

"But have you got any proof that it was David?" asked Luce.

"I've got this pen of mine..."

"That's not proof," Fen was quick to point out.

"No, I know it isn't, but let me ask you something. Did any of you lot tell David that my pen had been confiscated?"

We all looked at each other and shook our heads.

"And neither did I. So how did he know, then? How did he know that Mr Grote had *this* pen of mine? Tell me that." Rob looked round at us. My stirrings of unease had grown into a very uncomfortable feeling, but I didn't want to believe Rob. He must have been mistaken. The others all wore frowns, except Luce who was looking at Rob as though he was her latest hero.

"He could only have known if he was the one to dob on you," she said, dramatically finishing off Rob's case for the prosecution.

"Exactly," said Rob.

"A teacher would never give one person's property to another person," said Tash, "even if he did feel like rewarding someone. That would be really underhand and deceitful."

"I agree," said Fen, "but I think old Grote rewarded David in another way, by letting him be leader of the orchestra."

"What!" I screeched.

"Ssh, he's coming," Fen said.

"Don't trust him," was Rob's parting shot as he went back to his own table.

"Hi," said David, smiling up to our table.

"Actually, David, I'm really sorry, but I forgot I'm supposed to be visiting someone in hospital, so I've got to go." This wasn't strictly true because, like I said, I didn't really have to go till a bit later but I just needed to get away to think.

"Oh, I'll come with you if you want," David immediately volunteered.

"Limpet," said Andy under her breath. I heard her, though.

"No, the hospital only allows one visitor at a time, you see," I improvized.

"What Leah means, David," said Fen, quite forcefully, "is that she's visiting a very dear old lady – a close friend – and naturally she'd rather be on her own."

"Anyway, I'd better get going," I rushed on, because I could see Fen's eyes glinting angrily and David looking downcast again. "See you tomorrow."

"See you, Leah," everyone chorused, but David's voice came just a fraction after the others, and sounded sort of plaintive.

All the way home I thought about what Robert had said. I couldn't bear to think that David would just take the pen from Mr Grote. David wasn't like that. He was nice. The trouble was that I agreed with Tash that Mr Grote would never dream of actually giving Robert's pen to David, so David must have taken it. Maybe poor David was so desperate to be liked by someone that he *had* to go to these lengths to achieve it. Then another thought occurred to me. Maybe David had actually planned on getting the confiscated pen back afterwards so he could give it to Rob. That was how desperate poor David was for friends. I could understand someone doing a thing like that in desperation. It didn't seem too terrible to me. The others seemed far from understanding, though. They weren't jealous of my relationship with David, were they? No, that wasn't their style, to be jealous of a boy. I was very confused, and I stayed that way for the rest of the evening.

Dad drove me to the hospital again and on the way we bought some flowers. Dad was all for buying a big bouquet, but I said I thought Miss Farrant would prefer a small bunch and she'd once told me she loved purple and blue flowers, so I specially asked the woman in the florist's to put only purple and blue ones in the bunch.

When we arrived in the hospital car park, Dad

asked me if I'd rather that he came up to Miss Farrant's room with me, or waited in the car. I said I'd go to reception on my own and then I'd come out and tell him. I was trembling as I went into the hospital because I knew that I might be about to get some awful news. Reception seemed to be very busy. There were five people in front of me. I waited patiently behind them for my turn, but when not a single person had moved after at least three minutes, I ran out to the car, collected the flowers and told Dad that it was fine for him to stay in the car.

I wasn't sure if I was allowed to go straight up to Miss Farrant's room without telling anyone, but there was no turning back now. Just outside her door I stopped and braced myself, then I looked in through the pane of glass.

"Come to see Miss Farrant, dear?"

I swung round at the sound of the nurse's voice, and managed to murmur, "Yes."

"In you go then. She'll be pleased to see you. I'll put those lovely flowers in a vase for you and bring them in, all right?"

My shoulders must have been up by my ears I was so tense, but with these words, my whole body sighed itself back to normal and I entered Miss Farrant's room with a big smile on my face.

"Hello, dear. You look happy. Do you know, I'm such a lucky person, I'm surrounded by smiling faces all day long. Not a single nurse or doctor round here looks miserable. It's wonderful!"

Miss Farrant was propped up by pillows and I thought she looked a teeny bit better than yesterday, which lifted my spirits like mad.

"Look at these lovely flowers from your young friend, Miss Farrant."

The nurse put them where Miss Farrant could see them, then went out.

"All my favourites. I do appreciate that, Leah. Thank you so much."

I noticed there were two other vases full of flowers on the other side of the bed, and also two or three cards. I wondered who'd brought them.

"Ah, you've noticed those other flowers. They're from my niece. She finally came to see me, but to be perfectly honest, she didn't know what on earth to say to me. It's been a while since I've seen her, you see. And the white and yellow ones are from my neighbour, Mrs Anderson. I've had a few get-well cards too. You see the one with the cat on the front? That's from Ms Chambers!"

I practically shivered at the sound of that name. It made all my worries and anxieties come rushing back.

"What's the matter, dear? You look as though you've seen a ghost. I'm not dead yet, you know!" Miss Farrant chuckled at her joke, but I couldn't find it funny, and I didn't know how she could be so light-hearted about something so serious and so sad … and so … close. I could feel myself choking up. It hurt me so much.

"Come and sit down on the bed, dear. That's right, you hold my hand. Now, listen carefully. I've been wanting to have a heart-to-heart with you, because I don't want to pretend that everything's going to carry on the same as it is now. I think you know I haven't got very long to live. I'm pumped up to the eyeballs with painkillers, and it's time for me to die now, love. Come on, don't cry…"

I couldn't help it. The tears were rolling down my face. This conversation was too much for me to bear. "I don't want you to die," I wailed. "Oh, please don't die, Miss Farrant! I won't be able to bear it."

"You *will* be able to bear it. I want you to bear it for my sake. We've had a lovely time together, you and I. You've no idea how much happiness you've given me, Leah. You must always remember that. And another thing … I believe in heaven. Do you?" I couldn't speak for silent, choking crying, so I nodded. "Right, well, I think I'll sometimes be able to see you after I'm dead. I've always believed that. I think that when you're playing in concerts and things, or just whenever you happen to think about me, I'll *know* you're thinking about me and I'll be there to give you lots of encouragement and love. Do you think that's reasonable? Or do you think I'm a barmy old lady, full of funny ideas? Hmm?"

Miss Farrant's eyes were twinkling away at me as she squeezed my hand. But as well as the twinkle there was something deeper, something searching my face, as though looking for a glimmer of agreement with her theory.

"I'll think about you all the time," I whispered.

"I shouldn't do that, dear. You'll get very bored."

Suddenly I giggled. It just came out of my mouth without me expecting it to. It was the way Miss Farrant had said that last sentence, as though I'd said I was going to do nothing but eat and sleep for the next two weeks, or something.

"That's better. I've missed that giggle."

I managed to stop crying then. What Miss Farrant had said about being able to see me from heaven, and being there for me when I was thinking about her, comforted me. I felt really babyish having to be comforted like this, but it was the only thing that stopped me from crying. I suddenly made a decision.

"Miss Farrant, I'm in real trouble at school for something I didn't do."

"Tell me all about it, then."

So I did. It was tempting to tell her all about David and the pen as well, and the fact that I'd been taken out of my position as leader of the orchestra, but she was looking tired, so I decided just to stick to the burglary story. All the time I was talking I had the impression that Miss Farrant was feeling worse and worse, and at one point the nurse came back in and said that I'd better go because Miss Farrant needed to rest. It was Miss Farrant herself who said, "She'll just be a few more minutes, nurse, but could I possibly have my tablets?" The nurse looked unsure whether to grant this request, but in the end she did.

"Only two or three minutes, mind," she said at the door.

I finished with the scene in Ms Chambers' office and explained about the hairbrush and the stolen items. Miss Farrant looked very sympathetic and said how awful it must have been for me.

"Do you know what I think I'd do if I were you?" she then said.

"What?"

"I'd see Ms Chambers or Mrs Merle first thing in the morning and tell them the truth. You can explain why you didn't at first, because you thought they'd never believe you, then say that you've thought carefully about it, and decided that you have to tell the truth to help them find the person responsible for the theft."

"But they'll never believe me, I know they won't."

"I'm sure they can't possibly think that you did it, Leah. I mean, you're not exactly criminal material, are you?"

Miss Farrant was smiling, but I don't think she could have understood me properly, because I was so convinced that Mrs Merle and Ms Chambers were sure I'd done the burglary.

"They'll never believe me," I repeated.

"Do you think they believe you now?"

"No."

"Well, then you've got nothing to lose."

The nurse came in and said that she was sorry, but that I really had to go.

"You'll do what I said, won't you, Leah?" said Miss Farrant, and I told her I would. Very slowly and with a lot of effort, she then put her arms round me, and I kissed her goodbye.

"I'm coming to see you tomorrow," I told her, and I could feel the tears coming again. I blinked and blinked to make them stay back. I didn't want Miss Farrant to see how sad I was.

"Get your mum or dad to phone before you come, dear, then I'll have time to put my make-up on, all right?"

Again a giggle escaped my mouth because Miss Farrant never ever wore make-up, and the thought of her wearing it was so funny.

"Bye-bye, Leah. All my love, dear."

"And all mine," I managed to say, still without

crying. At the door I turned round. She was looking at me, and even though my tears were welling up ready to spill, I forced myself to smile and she smiled back. Then I went.

The nurse wanted to talk to me, but I was intent on getting away. I met Dad coming up the stairs.

"All right?" he asked.

"Not really."

The following morning I didn't want to go to school, but Mum and Dad said I'd be better off being occupied with work and my friends than sitting at home, mooching around and feeling sad. Kim was being really sweet to me. She's always been a lovely big sister to have around, but she was extra lovely this day. All the way to school she chatted brightly about things that I had to concentrate on. She went through pop group after pop group, making me list the boys or girls in order of preference, then she started on what her flat in London was going to look like when she left home, and I had to describe my dream home, and she said wouldn't it be great if we both lived in London and we could keep nipping round to each other's places, and go to the theatre and the pub together. She didn't leave me a second to think about Miss Farrant.

I even forgot about my resolution during that

walk to school. As soon as I left Kim, though, I started psyching myself up. I was determined to do as Miss Farrant had said, and go to see Ms Chambers. I would try and tell her the truth about Friday. After that I could only pray that she believed me. Miss Farrant seemed to think she would.

Andy came rushing up to me as I went into our registration room.

"How was Miss Farrant?"

"She seemed a tiny bit better. But it's hard to tell. She was propped up on her pillows, whereas yesterday she was lying down. She'd got a card from Ms Chambers, and loads of other cards, and three lots of flowers including mine."

"I'm glad she seemed a bit better, Lee. I was thinking about you yesterday evening."

Tears came into my eyes when Andy said that. I'd been all right until that moment, but suddenly I felt the awful lump in my throat coming back.

"I'm scared, Andy."

"Don't be scared, Lee... Sorry. I shouldn't have mentioned it. You looked fine when you came in." At that point David appeared. "Leah's a bit upset at the moment, David," Andy told him firmly, but that look of nobody-wants-me came over David and I couldn't help feeling sorry for him.

"I just came to see how your friend in hospital is," he said gently, to me.

Andy turned her back on him and whispered, "Yeah, sure!" as she walked over to her own desk.

"That was kind of you, David. She's about the same as yesterday. She's in a lot of pain – you know."

He looked so sympathetic. What *was* it with Andy and Rob?

"And I was wondering, do you want to come to my place after school?" David went on. "We could practise that piece for the festival if you want."

"Er … well, I could come for a bit, but then I'm going to visit my friend in hospital again."

"OK. I'd better go to registration. I'll see you later, then."

The moment he'd gone, Andy came back over to me, making it really obvious that she didn't want to be anywhere near David.

"Why don't you like David, Andy?" I asked her, trying not to sound too bothered about it.

"I don't know how *you* can still like him after what Rob said about his pen and everything."

"I thought about that, and I still feel sorry for David that he has to go to those lengths to get people to like him."

"Well, I don't trust him… Anyway, forget about him. Jaimini picked up a fantastic card trick from Mark in the café yesterday. She's going to show us all at morning break on the netball courts."

"Oh, great!" I said, then immediately remembered that I was supposed to be going to see Ms Chambers at break-time. "Actually, I've just remembered, I think there's supposed to be an audition session for that festival thing I told you about. I'll came down at the end of break, though."

The first two lessons leading up to morning break went amazingly slowly. My nervousness got greater and greater, until by the time the bell for break rang, I was a nervous wreck. I waited till the others had gone off to the netball courts, then I walked with shaky legs along the corridor to Ms Chambers' office.

For nearly a minute I stood outside the office, plucking up the courage to knock on the door. In the end I had to force myself, so the knock came out sounding really loud and impatient. Tensing up at the sound of my over-the-top knock, I waited with bated breath for the "Come in," that Ms Chambers always said quite softly. When I'd waited for a count of thirty I knocked again, more softly this time, and waited for another count of thirty. All this time I knew she wasn't in her office, but something made me stay there, just to make sure.

Eventually I decided to go and try the staffroom. Someone always answers the staffroom door. This time it was Mr Farmer, one of the French teachers.

"Um ... I was looking for Ms Chambers. She's not in her office."

"She's away, Leah. Can I help?"

My eyes widened. "She's away? When will she be back?"

"Friday morning."

"Not till Friday?" I closed my eyes, feeling full of despair.

"Are you sure that someone else can't help you with whatever it is?"

"Do you know when Mrs Merle will be back?"

"I believe that she's coming back at the beginning of next week."

"Thank you." I turned and walked miserably away. The staffroom door didn't close. At least, I didn't hear it close. I was right.

"Leah, what's the problem? Surely *one* of the teachers can help."

I didn't answer, just shook my head and kept walking towards the turning in the corridor with the phone in it. I had twenty pence in my pocket. There was a phone book beside the phone. I looked up Mrs Merle's number and dialled it. It rang and rang and rang. I let it ring twenty-six times before I put it down. When I did eventually put it down, I felt too hopeless to move so I just stood there staring at the front of the phone book, and wondering what to do next. A voice behind me made me jump.

"Leah, are you OK?" It was Robert Taylor.

"Yeah, I was just day-dreaming. I'm fine." I flashed him the best smile I could manage and went striding off to join the others on the netball courts. I didn't want to get into conversation with Robert, not even for a second. He was just trying to get me to go off David, and nobody was going to make me do that.

Chapter 8

I haven't mentioned it yet, but I've got this boyfriend called Oliver who lives miles and miles away. Oliver's family and my family have been friends for years, and until quite recently I just thought of Oliver as a friend, but I don't now because he's changed dramatically!

The only reason I'm mentioning him is because it's suddenly occurred to me that I haven't given him a thought for the last week, which is unusual for me. I normally think about him at least once a day. I suppose I've had so much on my mind lately that there hasn't been any room in there for Oliver as well.

It's funny, though, because in the past, even when I've been full of worry and problems, I've still thought about Oliver just as much as ever. I think it might be because of David. I mean, David *is* a boy, after all. I definitely don't have the same sort of feelings for David as I do for Oliver, though. In fact, I don't think of David as being any different from Andy or the rest of my friends. So it can't be David who's stopping me thinking about Oliver, can it? It's all very puzzling. And now I can add to my list of worries the fact that I have absolutely no desire to write to Oliver whatsoever.

One of our school rules is that pupils aren't allowed to leave the premises during the school day until they're in year eleven. But occasionally a teacher gives permission for a pupil to go into the town to get something as a favour for the teacher. After break I had tech, and my teacher, Mr Blundell, asked me if I'd go into town and get him some wood glue. I had to go the staffroom with him and get a bill slip. Mr Farmer was there and he gave me a very strange look, but I just turned away and probably went pink. I asked if I could take Andy with me and Mr Blundell said that was fine.

So Andy and I set off together and talked about Miss Farrant for a while. Andy was trying to help me think about the good times we'd had together, like the time when I introduced my guinea pig to Miss Farrant's and the two guinea pigs looked and sounded like two old ladies having a gossip because of the way they were standing facing each other, taking it in turns to squeak. The squeak itself was a mixture of high and low sounds just like the rise and fall of humans talking. Miss Farrant and I had been in hysterics, and we'd finished up recording the guinea pigs. I think I've still got the recording somewhere. I remember labelling the cassette SUNNY AND STUBBLES, which were the names of our two guinea pigs.

"Andy! Look!" I had stopped in my tracks, aghast to see Elizabeth Driscoll's son just ahead of us but going in the same direction. He'd turned his head sideways and it was definitely him. I'd recognize him anywhere. "Quick! Cross over! I don't want him to see me."

"Why not? I want to know what you did or said that was so wrong. I'm going to ask him."

"No, Andy, please don't. Please, for my sake."

I'm convinced it was only the fact that she felt sorry for me because of Miss Farrant that stopped Andy from rushing up to the man and demanding why he was always on my case. To my horror I suddenly realized that I'd been spotted. The man was crossing the road himself and looking at me in that urgent way that people do when they've got to grab an opportunity quickly before it slips away.

"Don't let him talk to me, Andy. I really do not want to talk to him!"

"Quick! Down here then!"

There was a little alley-way that I'd been down once before which was a short-cut to the post office and one or two other shops, just off the High Street. We shot down it. Andy turned round just before we bolted into the post office and said, "Don't worry, that lorry will have hidden us." I didn't dare look, but she assured me that there was a huge oil lorry that would definitely have blocked the man's view.

My heart was beating wildly, partly because we'd run so fast and partly because I was scared. Andy and I compared pulses and mine was about twice as fast as hers. She's much fitter than me and she doesn't scare as easily. When we judged it safe to, we emerged from the post office, having studied every single driving licence, passport renewal, road fund licence form, etc. in sight, so as not to draw attention to ourselves.

I was nervous the whole time after that and Andy had to get the wood glue and fill in the form, while I kept my eyes on the door to the shop. I've never wanted to be back on the school premises quite as much as I did just then.

"But why?" Andy persisted. "What harm can that man possibly do you? I felt quite sorry for him, actually. He's probably desperate to tell you nothing's the matter."

"I'm sure you're right, Andy. It's just that I can't forget the look in his eyes in the café."

"Talking of the café, are you going there after school? It's my turn to work."

"Er … I think I'll probably go straight home and find out how Miss Farrant is."

"Oh, right. So you're not going to David's place, then?"

I blushed, because I'd actually decided to go quickly to David's place before going home but I didn't want to admit this to Andy because she'd only start lecturing me on how sinister David is.

"Probably not," I said carefully. Andy looked at me, but she didn't say anything else.

The rest of the day was spent trying to avoid Rob, who seemed to be determined to track me down. I just knew he wanted to slag David off, and I was fed up with having to defend him. It was getting exhausting. In fact, the truth was that I really did not want to go to David's house after school. I just wanted to go to the café with my friends. It wasn't that I didn't like David, just that he was always hanging around me. Whereas I used to feel sorry for him, now I had to keep reminding myself that he'd got problems because his plaintive tone and his clinging ways just irritated me. When I got home I was going to ask Kim to phone the hospital because Mum and Dad wouldn't be home till later, and Miss Farrant had particularly said that one of them should phone.

Maybe if I managed to avoid David for the rest of the day I could pretend that I'd completely forgotten about going to his place after school. So now I was having to avoid Rob *and* David. This was getting silly. At lunch I said I was going to the loo. I chose my moment carefully when I knew the others had just all been, then I went to the phone to try and get hold of Mrs Merle. I crossed my fingers all the way down the corridor that she would be there, but once again I had to listen to ring after ring after ring.

As I was putting the phone down I saw David through a window of a classroom that had the door open. He was looking round, probably for me. I'd be glad when the day was over. The moment I'd had this thought I shook it out of my head, because I was determined never to wish my life away, not even a day of it. All the same it was a relief when the end-of-school bell went. Andy had already told me she was jogging down to the café, and she seemed really pleased when I said I'd jog with her.

"I thought you were going straight home, Lee."

"I was going to ask Kim to phone the hospital, but I think I'd better wait till Mum or Dad is home."

"So you're coming to have a drink with the others?"

I nodded and we jogged off quickly, which

suited me because it was the best way to lose both David and Rob. I knew the others would follow in their own time. I felt hot, red and exhausted by the time we arrived at the café, but Andy looked as though she'd just been taking a short stroll. We parted ways so that Andy could go in through the back door and I found a table for five and sat down to wait for the others.

The first to arrive were Luce and Rob. They came straight over to me and we all ordered Cokes from Jan. I wasn't too happy to see Rob but at least he was with Luce and she was chattering away, so that there was no time for Rob to start talking about David.

There was hardly anyone in the café at that moment so Jan stayed and chatted with us for a few minutes, which was good because it meant that I still didn't have to talk to Rob. The others arrived after a while, and guess who was trailing in their wake? The moment he saw me sitting there he looked so hurt, I felt terribly guilty.

"Fen said she thought you'd gone straight home," he said, turning his sad eyes on me, which made me feel even worse.

"Oh, David, sorry. I completely forgot!"

"I thought you must have done. Shall we go now, then?"

My eyes happened to meet Rob's at that moment and I could see that he didn't want me to go. For some reason it didn't irritate me this time, maybe because he didn't start getting heavy with me. In fact, he wasn't saying a word. His eyes were simply saying, *I don't want you to go.* I looked back at David. *His* eyes were saying *Please, Leah, you're the only friend I've got. You're not going to make me look a fool in front of everybody, are you?*

"Yeah, OK," I told David, before I could change my mind.

I was aware of Rob letting out his breath and taking a long time about it. The others didn't say a thing, but Fen looked round for Andy. I think she would have got Andy to come over and persuade me not to go, but unfortunately for Fen, Andy was nowhere in sight.

"Bye, everyone. See you tomorrow."

"Bye, Lee. See you tomorrow," they all chorused. I noticed Rob's voice hadn't joined in, though.

It didn't take very long to get to David's house. He lived in one of a row of terraced houses. It was really sweet, but very small and rather dark inside.

"Is your mum here?" I asked, realizing suddenly that I knew absolutely nothing about David's background.

"No, she's out at work. So is Dad."

"What time will they be back?"

"Not till after you've gone, I expect."

"I won't have time to practise the piece, I'm afraid, David, because I've really got to get back and phone the hospital."

"Well, why don't you phone from here?"

"Because it's got to be Mum or Dad that phone. They wouldn't give me any information over the phone. I'm too young."

"You could put on an older voice."

"No, I'd better not."

"But the festival is on Friday. Don't you want to practise your part?"

"Give me the music and I'll practise it at home and then we'll have a run through in school tomorrow or Friday."

"Do you want a drink?"

"OK."

We had been talking in the tiny sitting-room which we'd come into through the front door. There was no hall or anything. From the sitting-room we went down three steps into the kitchen which was also very small.

"It's a sweet little house, David. How many bedrooms are there?"

"Just two."

"It must be really cosy."

I secretly thought that I would find it very claustrophobic living in his house. Not because it was small, but because it was so dark. It seemed even darker because the furniture was dark as well and so were the curtains – dark brown and heavy.

"Can I see upstairs?"

"Yes, if you want."

I followed him up the steep, narrow staircase, which turned sharply in the middle, then we went up a step off the little square landing into David's room. It was very neat and tidy, which wasn't difficult because there was hardly any furniture. He'd got a lot of books and he'd also got a CD player in his room. The CD player looked somehow out of place, as though it had no right to be such a gleaming modern presence in that little dark room.

"That's the other bedroom," said David, reaching across the landing and touching a closed door. "And that's the bathroom."

That was obviously where the guided tour ended, because David was on the top stair ready to go back down again. But then the phone rang from downstairs.

"I'm just going to the loo," I said, entering the little bathroom which had a white wash basin, bath and loo, but dark brown rug and curtains. David went downstairs to answer the phone. Before I shut the door to the bathroom I noticed there was another door directly across the landing from the bathroom which was slightly ajar.

Curiosity got the better of me and I opened it.

There were more stairs behind it, only these were very narrow, steep stairs indeed. I could hear David's voice on the phone, and though I felt like an intruder I couldn't resist going up the stairs. They led me to a box room which was full of clutter. All over the floor were pictures and boxes and bags, bedding, a clock, an ironing board, loads of junk. My eyes roamed round and came to an abrupt stop. My heart felt as though it had also come to a standstill because I was staring at Mrs Merle's metronome and music box. They were definitely hers, I'd have recognized them anywhere.

The shock and horror I felt were stopping me from moving but when eventually I did move, I found my knees had turned to jelly and I could hardly manage the steps down to the landing. *Please let David stay on the phone for a bit longer to give me time to recover*, I prayed, but at that precise moment I heard the tiny ring that old-fashioned phones make when you replace the receiver. I arrived on the landing to see David looking at me from halfway up the first flight of stairs. He must have seen that I'd not come out of the bathroom, but he didn't say anything.

"I've got to go, David. Thanks for the drink, though … and for inviting me … and have you got the music?" I was beginning to gabble. *Slow down, Leah. Slow down.*

"Are you sure you've got to go? You've only just got here."

"Yeah, I know. I'm sorry."

I wasn't sorry at all. I was numb. He gave me the music and I only just managed to smile as I went. I made myself walk until I was out of sight, then I ran like the wind, and as I ran the numbness went, and in its place came a horrible eerie feeling. There was something wrong with David. There must be. But why should he take Mrs Merle's things? And did he deliberately set out to take those very items? So had he been inside Mrs Merle's house before? I thought I was the only pupil to have ever been at Mrs Merle's house. So the others had been right, and so had Rob. I could still see Rob's eyes looking at me in the café, and I could still hear that long outward breath of his. Fancy Rob caring so much about me.

Thoughts like these were rushing and jostling around inside my head, and I wasn't looking where I was going, so I ran slap bang into somebody walking in the opposite direction.

"Oh, sorry. My fault. I wasn't looking. Sorry." It was the man. *The man!* I gasped and set off again but he held on to my arm and stopped me from moving. I felt terrified. "Let go of me!"

"Leah, Leah, don't worry. I wouldn't dream of hurting you or anything like that. I just wanted to tell you not to worry. I know you think you said something terrible, that time in the café, and it seemed terrible at the time, but I realized straight after we'd left that it was a complete misunderstanding. I've been trying to tell you that ever since but you seem to have got it in your head that I'm some nasty evil person, and you keep running away."

I had been tugging at first to get away, then after a few seconds I had stopped tugging and he had immediately let go of my arm. Finally, I had looked at him and seen that he'd got quite a kind twinkly face, and it was obvious he couldn't hurt a fly. This was my second shock in one day. It crossed my mind that I must have been the worst judge of character in the history of the world, because first I'd got Rob and David wrong, and now I'd got this man wrong.

"I want to show you something that will explain everything." He got out a newspaper from his pocket. It was already folded back on page five so that only one article showed. At the top of the article was a picture. The picture was of Elizabeth Driscoll. "That's my mother."

"I know that now."

"But who did you think she was before, then?"

"Well, that was the problem. I mistook her for Anna Slater."

"Really? I think my mother would be flattered. You see, she's a violinist too, only nowhere near as famous as Anna Slater. But she does play in all sorts of concerts. This article was written after she'd played at quite a big venue, though. She'd felt very honoured to have been asked because there were one or two fairly well-known people playing that evening, and my mother had been pleased with the way she'd played. But then she saw this. And it completely shattered her confidence."

I quickly read the beginning of the article, which was only short. It said how badly the reviewer thought Elizabeth Driscoll had played her violin, and what a shame because the rest of the evening had been so good. It went on in this insulting way for a few more sentences and then I came to the final sentence.

"I suppose even the best violinists have 'off' days."

The words hit me, as I recalled exactly what I'd blithely said to Elizabeth Driscoll in the café that day: *I suppose even famous violinists have days off.* The two sentences were remarkably similar.

"We naturally assumed you were deliberately making a reference to this article. My mother thought you were trying to be clever and to make her feel small."

"But I'd no idea about this. No idea at all."

"I know. I realized that as soon as we left the place, and I felt really sorry for you. So did my mother. That's why I've been so intent on trying to track you down ever since. I wanted to tell you that there was nothing to worry about. Then, when I realized that you were scared of me, I didn't know what to do. I didn't want to make matters worse by appearing to be pursuing you but I just thought if I could talk to you for one minute, I could set everything straight."

"Well, I'm really relieved," I said, "only I still wish I'd never said a word in the first place. It's taught me a lesson. I'll always make sure I know who I'm talking to before I say things in future."

"Incidentally," he went on, "I know you won't believe me, but I thought your playing at that concert the other day was fantastic. I told my mother. She had to go home because she developed a migraine shortly after she arrived at the hall, otherwise she would have heard you herself."

"I played terribly at the concert! I was really embarrassed. Something put me off right in the middle."

"Yes, I realized that. I felt sorry for you. By the way, are you playing in the festival on Friday evening?"

He'd reminded me of David. "I'm not sure."

"Well, I should if I were you. You won't regret it. My mother will definitely be there, because she's organized the whole thing, and I know she'd love to hear you play. It's quite an important festival, I think you'll find."

He was looking and sounding very mysterious.

"In what way, important?"

"Aha! You'll have to see. Anyway, I'd better be on my way. I'm glad we've got everything sorted out, Leah."

"How did you know my name, by the way?"

"I heard one of your friends say it... Oh, and I'm Philip. See you Friday."

He carried on walking in the direction he'd been going, so it really had been sheer coincidence that we had come across each other, or that I had thrown myself at him, I should say! I was glad about the coincidence because now at least I had one less thing to worry about. As soon as I thought Andy would be back home from the café, I'd phone her and tell her all about David. It would be a long phone call because I'd have to tell her the whole story about Mrs Merle and Friday afternoon and the burglary and my awful interview in Ms Chambers' office.

It would be easier to tell Miss Farrant. She'd be able to advise me what to do next. I couldn't just go blundering in to Ms Chambers' office when she got back on Friday and tell her it wasn't me, it was David Laws. Too much time had gone by since it had happened, and anyway she'd need proof and we couldn't go marching round to David's house together. I didn't know how I was ever going to prove it. The problem was that it was *my* hairbrush that had been found inside the house. I was back to square one. Who would ever believe that I'd had nothing to do with the burglary?

I dropped David's music on the hall table, thinking that I'd somehow have to get out of playing with him because I couldn't bear the sight of him any longer. I remembered what Philip had said about his mother having to go home from the concert because she had a migraine. Maybe I could use the same excuse for not going to the festival. Mr Grote couldn't *make* me go, could he? I wouldn't really be letting David down either, because Mr Grote could play the accompaniment. Anyway, what if I was letting David down? Who cared? On the other hand Philip had said it was an important occasion and he'd looked as though it was something pretty exciting. I was curious. Perhaps it would be best to grit my teeth and play the stupid piano part with David and then never have anything more to do with him again. Yes, that was the best plan, but now I needed Kim.

"Kim," I called up the stairs. "Are you there?"

She appeared at the top of the stairs. "Hi, Leah."

"Can you do me a favour?"

Then I saw her face. "Are you all right, Kim?

Danny hasn't finished with you again, has he?" She looked all blotchy as though she'd been crying. I began to go upstairs, never taking my eyes off her face. I felt so sorry for her.

She put her hand out when I was on the sixth stair as if to stop me coming any nearer. Then she called out in a strained voice, "Mum, Dad, Leah's home."

And then I knew. I just knew. I turned in slow-motion as if in a dream. Mum and Dad were standing at the foot of the stairs. Mum put her arms out to me. "Come here, love."

"Tell me. Just tell me," I said in the faintest whisper.

Mum nodded slowly.

"She's died, hasn't she?"

Again Mum nodded, and I sat down slowly on the sixth stair.

Chapter 9

The audience is so still and quiet, you could have heard a pin drop. I'm trying. I'm trying so hard, but my fingers won't work. They're not playing what's written on the music. They're playing that tune again. I can't bear it. It's getting louder and louder, and I want to scream out, *"Look, I can do better than this!"* But I daren't scream because it might make the bomb go off. I can hear the countdown … five, four, three, two, one … *smash*!

"Leah! Leah! It's all right. You're dreaming."

Mum was leaning over the bed. I opened my eyes and couldn't work out what day it was or anything. I looked at my watch. Ten past nine. Ten past nine! Thursday!

"I'm late for school!"

I sat up and immediately felt so dizzy and strange that I had to flop back down again.

"How do you feel, love?"

I thought about it. How did I feel? I felt dizzy and strange. Anything else? Yes. I felt as though something was hanging over me, something dark and dull that was slowly coming down on to me and getting into my skin. It wasn't the dream. I was used to that now. I'd had the awful nightmare so often. It was something else. Then I remembered. Miss Farrant had died.

That's what Mum meant when she asked me how I felt. But what's the answer? There isn't an answer. You can't say "sad" or "quite sad" or "very sad". It's just something that takes you over and stops anything else from mattering. And you definitely don't want to talk about it.

"I'm not going to work today, Leah. I've rung in to tell them my daughter's not well. Can I get you anything, love? A cup of tea or hot chocolate? What about some cereal or toast?"

I shook my head and stared at the ceiling. This feeling wasn't the same as anything I'd felt before.

"I'll be downstairs. Bang on the floor with this walking stick if you want me."

My eyes were boring a hole in the ceiling. Mum crept out of the room as though I was asleep. I might as well have been asleep. I didn't feel as though I was awake. Miss Farrant had died in her sleep at midday the previous day. I got out of bed and walked shakily over to my bookshelves. There were cassettes on the shelves as well. One of them was marked SUNNY AND STUBBLES. I put it in my tape recorder, pressed play and went back to bed.

The recording was very clear. It had been so funny at the time to hear the two guinea pigs chuntering and chumming and squeaking away. Even now, it sounded just like a language, but I didn't laugh. Then Miss Farrant's voice came on the tape, followed by mine. I'd forgotten we had talked on this tape. I began to smile at the sound of our voices, and also at the realization that I had a reminder of Miss Farrant from when she was happy and well.

"It's amazing, isn't it? They sound so like humans!"

"What do you think they're saying?"

"'How do you do, my name's Sunny...' 'Oh really! Mine's Stubbles...' 'Fancy that! Stubbles! Though I must admit you do *have that look about you. Not being rude or anything, you understand.'"*

After Miss Farrant said that I giggled, then we both laughed. Then Miss Farrant said, *"What are they saying now? Go on, Leah."*

"They're saying, 'Hay isn't what it used to be, is it?...' 'Well, personally I prefer grass any day of the week...' 'Really? I've been meaning to ask you, do you live alone?' 'No, I live with my sister Candlewick but she doesn't get out much these days...'"

After that both Miss Farrant and I cracked up. This was followed by a bit more squeaking, then the recording finished. I got up, pressed rewind and played it through again.

Yesterday evening I had cried so many tears that my eyes had hurt, my head had ached, and my whole body had felt as though someone had pounded and pummelled me into a limp and lifeless rag. Mum had given me hot chocolate to drink and she'd put some whisky or something in it. It didn't taste very nice, but it helped me to sleep.

I spent the morning playing the tape over and over again, then I went back to sleep. When I woke up I read a chapter of a book that was far too young for me, but it was what I felt like reading. At lunchtime the phone rang. Mum answered it and came up to tell me it was Andy and the others phoning from school to find out how I was. Mum said she thought I was asleep, so she explained about Miss Farrant dying to Andy and said that I was a bit under the weather. I still couldn't work out if I was actually ill, or if I was just in this state because of the grief I felt. I don't think Mum knew either.

At quarter to four, when the others would have been just coming out of school, I still hadn't got up. During the afternoon I had finished my book and read another two books for primary school children. My brain didn't want to cope with anything for my own age group. I had thought about writing to Oliver. In fact, I'd even got as far as getting the paper out and writing *Dear Oliver*, but then I hadn't known what to write, so I'd dropped it on to the floor. After that I must have fallen asleep again, but when I woke up I noticed that the *Dear Oliver* paper was placed neatly on my dressing-table, so Mum must have come into the room and tidied it away.

At four-fifteen the phone rang. Mum called upstairs that it was Andy and did I want to take it in her and Dad's room? I did.

"Hi, Leah. I'm really sorry. You must be devastated."

"Yeah."

"Do you want company, or would you rather be on your own?"

"On my own ... for a bit... You don't mind, do you?"

"Course not. You know me."

"Yeah. Thanks."

"I'm glad she died peacefully."

"Yeah."

"If you're not in school, I'll phone you tomorrow, Lee. I'm thinking about you."

"Thanks."

"See you."

"Bye."

I think this must have been the only conversation ever to take place between Andy and me where she said more than me. Just talking seemed to use up so much energy, and energy was one of the things I was very low on. Next to phone was Tash. I asked Mum to say I was asleep. It wasn't that I didn't want to talk to Tash in particular, simply that I couldn't raise the energy to talk to anyone.

Tash was phoning on behalf of all the others. Mum seemed to be on the phone with her for ages. Afterwards, she came up to tell me that Peta had got a present for me. Apparently she wanted to bring it round personally. She'd been told that I was sad because a friend of mine had died and gone to heaven. Mum had told Tash to tell Peta that she could come round and see me when I was feeling a bit better. Danny, Tash's big brother, had sent his love, and so had Helen, Tash's mum. I expect Kim had filled Danny in on what an emotional mess I'd been the previous evening.

In the evening Kim sat with me for about an hour. She said lots of kind and thoughtful things, but I just lay there listening and hardly saying a word back. When Dad came home he came up with a pack of cards and played cards with me. In a way, this was easier because I hardly had to talk at all. I noticed that David didn't phone me. I wouldn't have spoken to him if he had done. My skin felt crawly when I thought about David. I went to sleep at eight o'clock.

On Friday morning I woke up feeling a bit better. My mind had lost its numbness and my body had regained some energy. All the same I loathed the thought of school. I didn't want to have to talk to people. I washed and dressed, then sat cross-legged on the middle of my rug and closed my eyes.

Can you hear me, Miss Farrant?

I don't know what I was expecting, but I was expecting *something*, just a feeling or something. There was nothing. I wanted to cry, but I knew I'd done enough of that. I was determined not to let anything drag me down. I was putting all my energy into getting myself up again. I would try again later. Meantime, I would have breakfast with the rest of the family. So I did. Everyone was delighted to see me at the breakfast table. Mum asked me whether I minded her going to work. Would I be all right on my own? I said I'd be fine, and I really thought I would be.

I played my violin for two hours that morning and loved it. In my mind I was giving Miss Farrant her own private concert. It made it worthwhile playing for someone. At lunchtime there was a knock on the front door. My heart beat more loudly because I couldn't think who it could be, unless it was a salesman or someone like that. I considered not answering the door, but decided that I would.

Standing on the doorstep was Rob Taylor.

"Just tell me to go away if you want, Leah," was his opening line. It completely flummoxed me because we hadn't even said hello and he was talking about going. I couldn't help smiling, and as I smiled it dawned on me that this was the first time I'd smiled since I'd heard about Miss Farrant's death.

"Come in, Rob. Did you escape from Cableden prison?"

"It did feel a bit like that, yeah. Andy told me not to come but I wanted to see you."

"I'm glad you came."

"I know you're feeling lousy and you don't want any visitors and... What did you say?"

"I said I'm glad you came."

"Why?"

His question took me by surprise. I didn't know the answer. I just was.

"I just am."

"I'm flattered." He smiled, and I thought how good-looking he was. I'd never noticed that before. He took his jacket off and chucked it over the arm of a chair; then he picked it up again, shot me a worried look and put it down slowly and neatly as though he'd been taking a liberty chucking his jacket about in someone else's house.

It was nice of him to do that. He *was* nice. I didn't know why I'd been so hard on him up until now. Well, I did know really. It was all because of stupid David Laws. If it hadn't been for that nauseating boy I would have got friendly with Rob Taylor much sooner and realized how good-looking he was, and how nice *and* how much I liked him...

And that's when it hit me. I fancied him! This was the reason I couldn't bring myself to write to Oliver. Rob had been in my mind all the time, I just hadn't allowed myself to believe it because I'd felt such a ridiculous sense of pity and protection for David.

"The thing is, I overheard old Grotey on the phone," Rob was saying. "I know you won't hear a word against David, but..."

"I'm off David," I said briefly.

Rob didn't make any comment, he just eyed me carefully.

"Grotey was talking about the festival to someone. I don't know who he was talking to, but he was arguing with this person. I heard him say, 'The fact remains, I haven't said a word to any pupils about the main purpose of the evening as far as Elizabeth is concerned.' Then he listened to the other person talking, but his face wore a look of irritation. Next he said, 'David is a boy who needs every ounce of encouragement he can get. His physical handicap alone...' Then the person must have interrupted and disagreed with him, because he said, 'But you said so yourself...' Then he sounded really puzzled and said, 'You specifically mentioned that in your notes... Well, he's not as talented as Leah, no, but I thought you felt that that girl needed taking down a peg or two...' Then he sounded *really* shocked and said, 'I don't understand this at all. I gave David her job as leader of the orchestra. I thought that's what you wanted me to do...' After that he sounded really worried and said, 'I can't change it now. It would be against the rules. Apparently Leah is playing the piano part. David asked her himself and she agreed. Oh dear, what a mess.'

"I couldn't listen in any more because Ms Chambers appeared behind me and told me to go outside. It was morning break, you see."

All that Rob had overheard Mr Grote saying on the phone had really shocked me and completely baffled me. I couldn't work out who it could have been on the other end of the phone who thought I needed taking down a peg or two. It was awful to think that someone thought I was cocky and conceited. I never meant to give that impression.

"Don't look so worried, Leah. I didn't mean to alarm you. I just kind of wanted to warn you. You see, I think David has got something to do with all this. I can't work out where he fits in, but I'm convinced that somewhere along the line, he does."

"So who do *you* think Mr Grote was talking to, Rob?"

"Well, at first I'd no idea, then I began to think it must be Mrs Merle, because he was talking about what was written in the 'notes', and I thought teachers usually give supply teachers notes about what they're teaching and what the pupils are like and everything."

"And what did you make of all that stuff about the festival?"

"I thought you might know what that was about. I've no idea, but the whole conversation sounded fishy to me, very fishy."

"I wish I'd never agreed to play the piano with David at the stupid festival, now."

"Well, don't then."

"I've got to. It's all arranged."

"You can't if you're ill."

"I'm not really ill. I'm just … sad."

"I'm sorry about Miss Farrant, Leah. Andy told me. That's another reason I came. I couldn't bear to think about you being sad all on your own. And also, I wanted to apologize for being so horrible to you over the pen in that first music lesson with Grotey. You see, it shocked me. Something kind of happened inside my head when you turned round. It was the sight of your face and your hair and everything. You looked so pretty, and I had to act horrible or Chris and Guy would have taken the mickey out of me. I felt like I was making my feelings really obvious, you see."

Rob looked very embarrassed all of a sudden. He got up and went over to the window. "Nice garden."

I could tell he wasn't interested in the garden at all. He just wanted to change the conversation because he thought he'd been too sentimental and girlie for a boy. But what boys don't realize is that girls don't think of it as being sentimental and girlie, they think of it as being really honest and kind. I suddenly wanted to let Rob know I liked him and that I appreciated his visit and his reason for coming. I walked over to him and rested my hand on his shoulder.

"Thanks for thinking about me, Rob. It means ever such a lot."

He turned towards me and put both arms round my waist and I wrapped my arms round his neck. We stayed in this hug for about five seconds, which is a long time. I was the one who pulled away first, but the embarrassed look had gone from Rob's face. He just looked very real. I know that's a funny way to describe how someone looks, but the thing is, *nobody* and *nothing* had looked real to me since Wednesday afternoon, and now suddenly I was coming alive again. Maybe a little part of me had died for a short while, when Miss Farrant had died, and somehow Rob had brought it back to life for me.

"Will you play me something on the violin?" he asked me out of the blue.

So I did. I played him my favourite piece. At the end he said, "Why don't you play *that* at the festival, instead of a tinpot piano duet?"

"I would if I was allowed to. But it's too late."

"I'm coming to the festival tonight. I don't normally go to things like that, but I want to be there if you're going to be there." I had been dying to ask Rob to come along but I hadn't dared, so I felt elated that he wanted to come anyway. "By the way, who is this Elizabeth person who's organizing the festival. What's the big deal about it?"

"I don't know what it's all about, but I gather it's being organized by someone called Elizabeth Driscoll, who's a violinist."

"So what do you think it is that Mr Grote was being so secretive about? You know, when he said that he hadn't said a word to the pupils about the main point of the evening as far as Elizabeth is concerned."

I had a flash of memory of Elizabeth Driscoll's son, Philip, telling me it was an important occasion. I wished I understood what was going on, I really did.

"I'd better be getting back," said Rob. "You *are*

definitely going to be there tonight, aren't you?"

I nodded. "If *you* are, yes."

And before I knew it, we were locked in one of those big hugs again. This time we both pulled away at the same time, because there was a knock at the door. So as I said goodbye to Rob and he went, I also said "hello" to Helen, Tash's mum, and Peta.

"If you're not feeling up to visitors, just tell us, and we'll go," Helen immediately said. "It's just that we were passing, and Peta has been desperate to give you this present."

"I'm feeling much better," I said, opening the door wider to let them in, while giving Rob a special smile as he went jogging back to school. Helen didn't make any comment about Rob. She's a very discreet person, Helen is, not at all gossipy.

"Open it up, Leah," said little Peta, hopping up and down with excitement as she thrust the package at me. "I fink you're going to really like it, cos it does crying too, like what you do, see." She had wrapped yards of Sellotape round and round it and it wasn't easy to unwrap. "And you can bofe cry togevver, see, and ven you can give it back to me at ve end of all the crying, cos it's mine really, see."

This speech was delivered very gravely. Peta was making it quite clear that whatever was inside this package was definitely not mine to keep. I had a good idea what I was going to find, if ever I got to the inside. And I was right.

"It's Conker, int it?" Peta exclaimed proudly and loudly as I pulled the nude doll out of the final wrapper.

"Thank you very much, Peta. It's very kind of you. But where are her clothes? Isn't she cold?"

"No, cos all her crying makes her cloves all wet so I took vem off. Have you finished crying now, Leah?"

"Yes, I think I have," I told her, trying not to laugh. Helen rolled her eyes at me, as if to say, "Three-year-olds!'

"OK. I'll have Conker back now then." And with that she more or less snatched the doll from my hands.

"Oh, Peta! You can't give someone a present and then take it back straight away," Helen said in a strict voice.

"I don't mind," I mouthed at Helen.

"She's got to learn," Helen mouthed back.

"Tell you what, I'll definitely give her back tomorrow. How about that, Peta?" Peta looked rather doubtful and nodded reluctantly. "Would you like a cup of tea, Helen?"

"No love, thanks all the same. We're on our way to the garden centre. I'm glad you're feeling so much better. Give my love to your mum and dad, and I'll see you soon."

Mum came home early that day to check that I was feeling all right. She broke into a big beam when she saw me. "My goodness, *you* look transformed. What's happened?"

I knew what had happened but I didn't really want to tell Mum how I felt about Rob. I didn't want to tell anyone. I just wanted to hug it to myself. The phone rang shortly after that, and Mum answered it. I couldn't hear what she was saying or who it was or anything, but when she'd finished the call she came in to me and said, "That was Mr Grote from school. He was concerned that you weren't going to be well enough to play at the festival tonight. I had to be honest and say that I didn't actually know anything about it, but he's explained it all to me and I said you would be there. Is that all right?"

"What exactly did he explain?"

"Just about it being organized by someone called Elizabeth Driscoll and how all the local schools are entering two items. I gather you're playing the piano with a boy called David on his violin. Is that right?"

I nodded.

"How come you're not playing your violin?"

"David persuaded me to play with him, but I regret saying yes now."

"Oh well, never mind. You can't be kingpin at every concert and festival, can you?"

Somehow, it didn't matter so much any more. I had Rob now. He hadn't directly asked me to go out with him, but he didn't need to. This was the end of the "Oliver" chapter in my life. It was ridiculous having a boyfriend who lived so far away anyway.

I had a bath and put on the long skirt which I often wore for concerts. I was tempted to put some make-up on but I didn't, because I don't like make-up and I've always said I wouldn't wear it just because other girls do. Even my sister, Kim, wears hardly any.

It was seven-twenty-five when Mum, Dad and I went into the massive auditorium where the festival was taking place. The whole hall was packed out. There seemed to be hundreds of people there. Mr Grote was beckoning to me from the front, so I left Mum and Dad and went to see where I was supposed to sit.

"How are you feeling, Leah?" he asked me in quite a kindly voice, I thought.

"Much better, thank you," I told him, then I saw David. Immediately that horrible creepy-crawly feeling came over me. I wondered what was going on inside David's head. Goodness knows why I'd ever felt sorry for him. I suppose because of his hand, and his lack of friends. I had no idea whether he guessed that I had gone up to his attic and seen Mrs Merle's music box and metronome. I didn't even know if David would expect me to recognize those things even if I had seen them. All I knew was that David was different towards me. He wasn't vastly different, just subtly so.

"Hi, Leah. I hope we'll manage all right, when we haven't had the chance to play the piece together. Oh, yeah, I'm sorry about your friend dying."

He was gazing round as though looking out for more interesting people than me, and I could tell he couldn't care less about my friend dying. I hadn't even played the piano music once at home. I'd just glanced at it and seen that it was very easy indeed. I would be able to sight-read it without any problem. Sight-reading means playing without having to practise at all. It's one of the things that all instrumentalists have to learn to do.

Thank goodness, one of the organizers of the festival asked Mr Grote to help put some music stands out at that point, and David followed them both and started helping, too. I watched David and a peculiar feeling came over me. Something was wrong, but I couldn't work out what it was. Then it hit me. The music stands were the folding sort, and they're really stiff and difficult to open out. It takes quite a lot of force, yet David was coping easily. His right hand was gripping tightly while his left hand wrenched and pushed.

There was absolutely nothing the matter with David's hand at all!

Maybe it's just got better, I quickly told myself, but it all seemed too convenient. I shivered and looked away. David had definitely realized that I didn't feel sorry for him any more. I hadn't even tried to hide the distaste I felt for him.

My eyes roamed over the audience. Elizabeth Driscoll was sitting in the front row. She wasn't looking at me. She was watching as the organizers put the final touches to getting the stage ready. Her son, Philip, was moving the piano with the help of another man. Mum and Dad were about halfway back. Mum gave me a little wave. Then I saw Andy and the others. They were all sitting in a row. They must have spotted me at exactly the same time as I spotted them because they all suddenly rose to their feet and came wading through everybody to get to me at the front. There was still a lot of chatter and noise going on, so it didn't matter.

They fell on me like a load of crows swooping on a dead animal.

"Are you all right, Lee?"

"We've been thinking about you all the time."

"Guess what! Rob Taylor really likes you. I know. I saw your name inside his pencil case." This was from Luce. I tried not to react.

"What are you playing tonight?" Jaimini asked.

"Some horrible piece with David. I can't get out of it, otherwise I would."

"I'm glad you've come to your senses about that spooky boy," said Fen, probably noting my sour expression.

"What I can't understand is why you're not the main one playing?" Tash said. "It's obviously a very important festival with all these schools represented here, and look! Even Ms Chambers is here."

My heart missed a beat when she said that. Although I hadn't exactly put the burglary and the fact that I'd felt wrongly accused to the back of my mind, I'd somehow managed to make it seem less important than it really was. But now that I knew that Ms Chambers would be watching me play and thinking about me being a thief at the same time, I felt sick.

And that's when I spotted her. She was sitting right near the front with Mrs Merle. The two of them were deep in conversation together. They looked so serious. I just knew they were talking about me.

And where was Rob? My eyes flew round the whole audience as a big feeling of panic started to take me over. *Rob, where are you when I need you?*

Chapter 10

Suddenly a hush descended on the auditorium and the girls sneaked back to their places. I sat down in the front row in one of the RESERVED FOR PERFORMERS seats. David didn't sit near me, thank goodness.

The first school to perform was Gradian Comprehensive, which has a very good reputation for music. The choir sang really well, but I couldn't appreciate it because all I wanted to do was turn round to see if Rob had arrived. The very second the conductor's arms dropped to his sides I craned my neck round and half stood up to see better. There was no sign of him at all.

Elizabeth Driscoll was making for the stage. I wondered what she would say. So did the whole audience, judging from the complete silence that descended over the auditorium.

"Welcome everybody," she began. "It's

absolutely wonderful to see such a vast audience. Can you hear me at the back there?"

A few people called out from the back that they could hear, which gave me a good excuse to turn round again.

"We've just heard from the Gradian Comprehensive School choir, and if that performance was anything to go by, I think we're in for a wonderful evening. I've always known that we have a lot of very accomplished young musicians in the area, and it's a wonderful treat for me to be able to get so many of them here under one roof tonight. What I haven't as yet revealed to you is that my intention is to offer a special award at the end of this evening to just one of our entrants. I feel very lucky to be going on a short musical tour to Vienna next month and I should like to invite this evening's award winner to come along with me as my guest. There will be one concert in Vienna at which they will be able to play and the rest of the tour should be of tremendous cultural interest, as well as being a wonderful experience for whoever comes along."

She paused at that point and smiled around to see what the reaction was. It was clear what the audience felt because they burst into loud applause. As she had been talking, though, my heart had been sinking bit by bit, until by the end of the speech, it was somewhere under the floorboards. Now I knew why the evening was so important. It was probably one of the most important musical occasions I had ever been to, but there was absolutely no chance whatsoever that I would win the award because I was only playing a pathetic little piano part that wouldn't show off any musical skills whatsoever.

If only Mrs Merle had never been away, Mr Grote wouldn't have been at our school, David wouldn't have been promoted to golden boy of the century, I wouldn't have gone round to Mrs Merle's house, nobody would be accusing me of burglary, and Mrs Merle would have got me to play a violin solo that would have at least given me a chance of competing for the award. As it was I wasn't even in the running. If only I could go to Mrs Merle and beg her to let me play my solo. But there was no way I could do that. Mrs Merle wouldn't be interested in encouraging a thief. Mrs Merle even thought I needed taking down a peg or two. Why? Why?

I turned round once more and saw that not only was Rob not here, but Dad had gone. Things were getting worse, not better. Elizabeth Driscoll had finished talking and had returned to her place. A girl from Gradian Comp was playing a cello piece. She had long hair and I kept worrying that it was going to get tangled up in her bow, but somehow it never did. The other Gradian Comp entrant was a boy playing the piano. He played a very fast piece by Schubert. There were a few slips in it but it was still very good. I noticed that Elizabeth Driscoll and the two people on either side of her, one of whom was her son, were writing things down all through the performances.

There were three more schools before the interval. All the items were good, but one of them was brilliant. It was a girl playing a euphonium, which is like a small tuba. I've never heard anyone of that age play a brass instrument so well. When she'd finished the audience clapped and clapped. Everyone, including me, could tell that this girl was very gifted. Her name was Hannah. "Lucky you, Hannah," I whispered under my breath, because it would take an incredibly talented person to give a better performance than the one we'd just heard.

The moment the interval was announced I found myself surrounded by Andy and the others. Trying to be as subtle as possible, I kept scanning the hall for any sign of Rob, but there was none.

"Leah, this is so unfair," Luce launched in indignantly. "You should be playing a violin solo. If Mrs Merle had been at school, she would have made sure you were. Why don't we go and explain to her now, that Mr Grote didn't realize that you are so much better than David? She's the proper music teacher. He's only a supply. He doesn't know anything."

I was expecting Jaimini or one of the others to tell Luce not to be so dramatic but not one of them did.

"Luce is right," said Fen.

"Absolutely," said Andy.

"No! No, I mean, you can't do that," I stammered, feeling petrified that Andy might approach Mrs Merle at any second.

"Why not?"

"Because it's too late. We're only allowed two entries per school. It wouldn't be fair on the other schools, if we had three."

"We wouldn't have three. We'd have two, same as everyone else," said Andy.

"But it wouldn't be fair to drop the girls playing recorder..."

"We'd explain to Mrs Merle that David was going to let our school down and that it should be you instead of him," Fen said.

"She'd never agree to that."

"Why not? You know how fond she is of you. We'd just tell her old Grotey dumped you as leader of the orchestra, and put David in your place. Mrs Merle would go spare if she heard about that. She'd soon get things changed around so that you could play the violin."

"But I haven't even got my violin..."

"You could borrow one."

"It's not the same."

"Stop making excuses, Leah. What's the matter with you? It's almost as though you don't want the chance to go to Vienna."

"Oh, I do, really I do. It's just that..."

"What?"

All five of them had been taking it in turns to fire all these things at me, and I was running out of excuses. At some point I was going to have to tell them the truth. I should have done it ages ago. The trouble is, the longer you leave things unsaid, the more difficult it is to finally say them.

"It's a long story," I said in a sigh, "but I don't think Mrs Merle likes me any more. She thinks I've done something ... bad ... but I haven't... Oh, it's all too complicated to explain ... sorry."

"Leah, I knew there was something else on your mind," said Andy softly. The others didn't say a word. I'd well and truly brought their great plans for me winning the award to a grinding halt. I looked across to where I'd seen Mrs Merle sitting with Ms Chambers and saw, to my shock, that *Rob* was talking to them both. Mrs Merle's eyes were very wide and Ms Chambers had her hand on her chin, with her forefinger tapping her lip. She often did this when she was deep into a problem. This was her pose for trying to solve something. I wondered what on earth Rob was saying.

"Take your seats, please, ladies and gentlemen," came a deep voice over the mike. Rob looked in my direction and our eyes met. He broke into a smile, a special smile just for me, then went to sit down further back. Mrs Merle moved over to where Mr Grote was sitting and sat down beside him, looking very grave. Dad, I noticed, was back in his place beside Mum. I saw Fen's mum sitting with Jan, just behind Mum and Dad. Fen's mum and Jan are sisters and often go out together. They're very close.

It seemed strange to see Jan here at an event like this. I didn't think it was her scene. She caught my eye and gave me a thumbs-up sign. How embarrassing. She must have thought I was going to play some wonderful solo, when all I was about to play was something I could have played four or five years ago. Seeing Jan there made me realize how much I'd missed the café. I wished that everything could go back to normal. I wanted to be an ordinary, happy girl working once a week at a café where all my friends worked. The only good thing that had happened recently was Rob.

For the next two items I did nothing but day-dream about Rob. I've no idea whether the performances were good or not. I never heard a single note! I joined in the clapping like a zombie, but then I suddenly realized there was only Gemma and Alex playing their recorder duet before my duet with David. I couldn't wait till the whole concert was finished and we could all go home. When I suddenly caught Ms Chambers' eyes on me, I quickly looked down again. She was staring straight at me, and her finger was still tapping her lip.

Gemma and Alex played their recorders really well and everybody clapped like mad. I glanced over at Mrs Merle, expecting to see her smiling and clapping away, but she was deep into conversation with Ms Chambers. And now it was my turn. A horrible wave of nervousness came over me. Why was I nervous? I was usually only nervous when I was playing something difficult and I was worried that it would go wrong.

David and I didn't even look at each other as we went on to the stage. I played an A on the piano for him to tune his violin, then a D. He was ready to go on to tuning the other two strings but his A and D were still flat and he obviously hadn't realized, so I whispered to him. In the end, when he was making it worse not better, he handed the violin to me and I tuned it quickly. A titter ran through the audience when I did this, and I didn't like it. I felt my cheeks flaming. They probably thought I was showing off. No wonder Mrs Merle thought I needed taking down a peg or two. David went back to the centre of the stage and I put the music on the piano stand.

It was from the very first second we started to play that I felt the dizziness creeping over me. You see, the melody line of my piano part was the very tune that I had been playing in my nightmare. My eyes were having difficulty focusing on the music and when I looked at my hands I saw that they were shaking. My cheeks didn't feel red any more, they felt white. Oh, no! This is it! This is the nightmare. Only now I'm actually living it! My gaze turned to Elizabeth Driscoll in the middle of the front row, but all I could see was Anna Slater. Something inside me felt as though it was about to explode. I couldn't go on. I couldn't play another single note of this music. I hated it. *I hated it!*

Any second now, I'd hear that voice counting down. I was ready for it, but instead I heard another voice – a soft, gentle voice.

"Don't worry, Leah. I can see you. I can hear you," said Miss Farrant.

The music came crashing down around me and then someone's arm was around me. "Miss Farrant, you *are* here," I said.

The next thing I knew, I was being jostled and helped and carried through the dark blur into a quiet place. Then I was sitting in an armchair in a room I didn't recognize.

"Are you all right now?" That was Mum's voice.

"What happened?"

"You fainted."

"I ruined the piece, but you see I couldn't play because..."

"Ssh, don't talk. It doesn't matter about the piece."

"Where's David?"

"Gone home." That was Mrs Merle's voice. I looked up, shocked.

"Don't look so worried, Leah. It's all sorted out. I know it wasn't you."

I flopped back in the armchair and looked at Mum to see what she made of this.

"I've been explaining everything to your mum. I'm only sorry that you've had such a difficult time lately."

"Why has David gone home?"

"Because I had words with him."

"I don't understand."

"To start at the beginning, I've been on jury service all week. That's why Mr Grote took over. It was supposed to be another supply teacher but she fell ill at the last minute, so Mr Grote came into school very unprepared because it was all so quickly arranged. I had made some notes about the music lessons for him which I gave to him at the weekend. What I didn't know was that David had been into my house on the Friday evening and added to them. He's been to my house before, you see, Leah, because I've been giving him some extra help with his music. He must have seen the notes I was preparing, and sneaked in on Friday to tamper with them. I didn't realize that anything fishy was going on until I spoke to Mr Grote on the phone this morning, about the festival. I couldn't understand why he hadn't put *you* in to play tonight.

"The more we talked, the more we both realized that whatever notes Mr Grote had read were not the notes *I* had given him. In the end he read out the sheet about you and David over the phone. Well, I couldn't believe my ears, and we could only assume that David had been responsible, because the notes were very damning about you, Leah, and very positive about David. David had even made up an injury to his hand." I gasped when Mrs Merle said that. I didn't think I'd ever felt such contempt and revulsion for anyone in my life as I did for David at that moment.

"Mr Grote confronted David, and he denied having gone into my house, but there was no other way he could have got hold of the notes. I remember telling him once about the metronome and music box, and how much you liked them, so he knew exactly what to take. Ms Chambers and I had never thought for a moment that you had stolen my things, Leah. We just needed you to admit you were in my house, because of the hairbrush, and in case you'd seen something. Then when you wouldn't admit it, we felt baffled."

"I didn't dare admit it. I thought everyone was against me. I thought you'd be sure to accuse me of burglary if I admitted that I'd been inside your house. I don't think I could have been thinking straight at that time. But then after school on Wednesday I saw your music box and metronome in David's attic. He didn't know I'd seen them. I thought of telling you, but then I thought you'd never believe me, because of my hairbrush. The only reason I was in your house was because I was upset about not being the leader of the orchestra any more, so I came to see you. I thought you'd be able to cheer me up. Your back door was open and I didn't know you were on jury service. I thought you were ill in bed, and so I went upstairs in your house, calling to you all the way. Then, when I realized there was no one there, I quickly went."

"I'd come home from court by then but gone out to the shop. My head had been so full of the court case that I'd stupidly left my door unlocked."

"I would have told you that I'd called round, of course, but I couldn't because of the burglary. I didn't know what to do, and I asked Miss Farrant's advice. She told me to explain the whole thing to Ms Chambers, so I went the very next day to find her at school, only Mr Farmer said she was away for two days. I even tried to phone you, but there was no reply. Then … then Miss Farrant died, and…"

"Miss Farrant obviously wasn't convinced that you would tell Ms Chambers because when Ms Chambers got back from her two days away, there was a message on her answer-phone from Miss Farrant, explaining the whole story."

I was silent for a moment, thinking about this. What an amazing person Miss Farrant had been!

"But how did *you* know it was David when you didn't have any proof?" I then asked.

"We didn't know. That's why our hands have been tied. Until this evening, that is."

"This evening? What happened this evening?"

"Well, Robert Taylor had apparently suspected David of not being quite as he appeared, and he'd also overheard Mr Grote talking on the phone to me. Robert was very worried on your behalf, Leah, and felt that it was unfair that you weren't playing your violin tonight. He came to talk to me in the interval, and it came out in conversation that I live in the same road as Robert. By pure chance he happened to mention that he'd seen me coming out of David Laws' drive this evening. I didn't know what on earth he was talking about, but it turned out that Rob thought David lived where I live because he'd seen him go round the back of my house on Friday evening and come out a few minutes later."

"That's incredible," I breathed. "Fancy Rob spotting David! If only I'd told Rob all about everything ages ago."

"Never mind. It's all come out now. We haven't had time to question David properly, but he gave the game away by saying he didn't know anything about a music box when nobody had actually mentioned that it was a music box that had gone missing. David knows Elizabeth Driscoll, you see, and she had made the mistake of telling him that there was a special prize for the most promising young musician of the evening. David has been determined to win the prize right from the word go, but you were in his way, Leah."

"So, all his friendship and everything was all to stop me playing solo tonight?"

"No, I don't think so. He's a very mixed-up boy, apart from all that," Mrs Merle said. "He's always trying to make people like him. He makes things up, but then he starts to believe the things himself. He needs ... help."

I nodded, thinking about his hand. Had David believed his hand really was injured when he'd told me that story about it? Then there was the pen. He must have been desperate to get Robert and the others to like him, the lengths he'd gone to over the torch-pen.

"There's one thing I still don't understand," I said. "If Mr Grote didn't get the notes about me and David until the weekend, how come he dropped me from orchestra before that?"

"Apparently David informed on Robert Taylor about a pen or something, and then got chatting to Mr Grote, and convinced him that I was on the point of swapping people around in the orchestra. So Mr Grote decided to let David be the leader. He had no intention of keeping him as leader, until he read 'my notes'!"

I listened in disbelief. What a sad, underhand boy David really was.

"We're only just getting to the bottom of the whole thing now, Leah, but the point is," continued Mrs Merle, "our school is allowed another entry because that duet never quite got off the ground, so if you're up to it, I'd like you to play your violin. Mr Grote would like to hear you, too. He's never heard how you really play, Leah."

"But I haven't even got my violin," I said.

"Yes, you have. Robert persuaded your dad to go home and get it. That boy was absolutely determined that you should play tonight, Leah."

So, that was why I was standing on the stage with my violin at the very, very end of the whole festival. Elizabeth Driscoll's son, Philip, had made a brief announcement about the fact that my solo was to replace the duet which had had to be abandoned earlier on. I didn't feel at all nervous. I still felt peculiar, as though I wasn't really there. It was that nightmare that did it.

How could I have known that I was going to be playing that very tune at a concert? Or was it the same tune? Had everything just got all mixed up in my mind so that I thought I was in my nightmare? That's what Mum had said. She thought that Miss Farrant's death had affected me more deeply than anyone realized, and that combined with everything else I'd had to cope with, my mind had sort of flipped.

I lost myself in my violin solo. It was my favourite piece, the one I'd been practising at home that morning. I didn't need the music because I had memorized it. It was a very slow, sad piece of music and I played it from the bottom of my heart especially for Miss Farrant, but even though it was so sad, it didn't make *me* sad. Miss Farrant had said that she thought that if I wanted her at any time, she'd be there for me, and as I played my solo, I really felt as though she was. If I'd had that thought yesterday, I would probably have started crying but I was past that now. It was as though I'd finally woken up from my bad dream. Well, in a way, that was true, wasn't it?

The applause shocked me. I'd forgotten about all the people there. I'd been thinking that it was just me and Miss Farrant but as I looked round into the smiling faces of the audience, I could see Mrs Merle and Ms Chambers, Mum and Dad, Mr Grote, Elizabeth Driscoll and her son, all my friends, Jan and Dee, Kim and Danny... But where was Rob? My eyes flew round the rest of the audience, and then I saw him. He'd moved to the front and was leaning against the wall, clapping away.

I started to leave the stage, making my way towards Rob, but Elizabeth Driscoll stopped me. She told me to stay on the stage and everyone went quiet.

"I think you know what I'm going to say," she said with a big smile to the audience, and they all broke into applause again. I wished they'd be quiet because I wanted to hear what she *was* going to say. I wanted to know who was going with her to Vienna. The audience seemed to be clapping for ever, so I whispered to Elizabeth, "What *were* you going to say?"

"Don't you know?" she whispered back.

I shook my head.

"You've won the award. If you can, I'd like you to come with me to Vienna!"

I couldn't believe my ears. In fact, I *didn't* believe my ears. "Are you sure?" I asked her.

"Quite sure," she smiled.

I wanted to hug her, I felt so happy.

"I'm sorry about what I said, by the way."

She laughed. "I'm sorry I reacted as I did. It was stupid of me. I sent Philip to try and find you and tell you not to worry, but you kept running away from him and he didn't want to frighten you even more. You're a very gifted girl, by the way, Leah. Very gifted."

And very lucky, I thought, as the audience at last stopped clapping and I left the stage.

Once again Luce and the others swooped upon me, only this time it was to congratulate me. Mum and Dad and Jan and Dee came to join the circle, along with Mrs Merle, Mr Grote and Ms Chambers. Rob hovered uncertainly on the outside, until Dad drew him in.

"I think a celebration is called for, don't you?" said Jan, smiling round at everyone.

"Yes!" came the enthusiastic answer from Luce and the others.

"Come on, then. Let's go to the café," Jan said, and another cheer went up.

For me, when she said that, it was like the last piece of a big jigsaw puzzle falling into place. I felt back to normal. Leah Bryan, one of the Café Club. There was just one difference, but nobody knew yet. Rob and I gave each other special, secret smiles.

"Isn't it great that Rob and Leah are going out with each other, Mrs Merle?" said Luce.

"Yes, it certainly is," said Mrs Merle, and everybody else nodded and smiled. So I think perhaps I was wrong about nobody knowing, don't you?

Join

Would you and your friends like to know more about Fen, Tash, Leah, Andy, Jaimini and Luce?

We have produced a special bookmark for you to use in your Café Club books. To get yours free, together with a special newsletter about Fen and her friends, their creator, author Ann Bryant, and advance information about what's coming next in the series, write (enclosing a self-addressed label, please) to:

The Café Club
c/o the Publicity Department
Scholastic Children's Books
Commonwealth House
1-19 New Oxford Street
London WC1A 1NU

We look forward to hearing from you!